D0873289

THE BOY WHO
SET THE FIRE

Also by Mohammed Mrabet

The Lemon
Translated from the Moghrebi by Paul Bowles

Love with a Few Hairs
Translated from the Moghrebi by Paul Bowles

M'Hashish
Translated from the Moghrebi by Paul Bowles

Paul Bowles & Mohammed Mrabet

THE BOY WHO SET THE FIRE

& Other Stories

Taped & Translated from the Moghrebi
by Paul Bowles

CITY LIGHTS BOOKS
San Francisco

First City Lights edition, 1989

Cover drawing by Mohammed Mrabet. Courtesy of the R. Berman
Collection.
Cover design by Patricia Fujii

Grateful acknowledgement is given to the editors of the following
publications where some of these stories originally appeared:
*Antaeus, Armadillo, Bastard Angel, The Great Society,
Mediterranean Review, Omphalos, Rolling Stone,* and *Transatlantic
Review.*

Library of Congress Cataloging-in-Publication Data

Mrabet, Mohammed, 1940-
    The boy who set the fire & other stories / Mohammed Mrabet; taped
and translated from the Moghrebi by Paul Bowles.
        p.   cm.
    ISBN 0-87286-230-5 : $6.95
    I. Bowles, Paul, 1910-   II. Title.
PJ7846.R3A24 1988
892' .736--dc19
                                                        88-16864
                                                        CIP

City Lights Books are available to bookstores through our primary
distributor: Subterranean Company, P.O. Box 10233, Eugene, OR
97440   (503) 343-6324. Our books are also available through library
jobbers and regional distributors. For personal orders and catalogs,
please write to City Lights Books, 261 Columbus Avenue,
San Francisco, CA 94133.

CITY LIGHTS BOOKS are edited by Lawrence Ferlinghetti &
Nancy J. Peters and published at the City Lights Bookstore,
261 Columbus Avenue, San Francisco, CA 94133.

TABLE OF CONTENTS

THE BOY WHO SET THE FIRE

SI MOKHTAR

A VERY OLD RIFFIAN who lived in Boubana had four sons. Before he died he divided his land equally among them. The three younger men thought only of selling their share, but Si Mokhtar, the eldest, loved the place where he lived, and did not want to see it change. And so he bought his brothers' shares from them, and went on living in his father's house.

The orchard had all the hundreds of pear trees that his father had planted during his long lifetime in Boubana, and there were six deep wells on the land. In the garden Si Mokhtar grew the vegetables he needed for himself and many more. What he did not need he sold. Behind the house there was a clearing that always had been there, because nothing would grow there, and beyond that he had built a fence out of high canes and covered it with vines. The fence hid a patch of kif and a patch of tobacco. Between the two he had left a small place where he could sit.

Si Mokhtar had two big dogs. The white one was chained at one end to guard the kif, and the black one at the other to guard the tobacco. A farmer who lived nearby came every day to help him with his work. During the season when the pears ripened, the man would come with his donkeys each morning before daybreak, and he would find the crates of pears that Si Mokhtar had piled the day before, ready to take away. He would put them on the donkeys and ride off to the city. When he had sold them all, he would buy Si Mokhtar's food and two kilos of horsemeat for the dogs, and set off for Boubana. He would get back to the house as Si Mokhtar was waking up.

9

Each day it was the same. Si Mokhtar would open the door and step outside. The farmer would go past him into the kitchen with the food, and Si Mokhtar would walk to the well, fill a pail with pure cold water, and begin to wash. When he had finished and dried himself he would lift his face to the trees and say good morning to them. I'm still alive for you, he would tell them. And hamdul'lah, you're still alive for me. Then he would go inside and light the fire and put on the water for tea. For his breakfast he always ate a loaf of fresh brown bread spread with sheep's butter and wild honey. Si Mokhtar was no longer a young man, but he was still healthy. The teakettle stayed on the fire and the farmer sat and ate with him. But he would eat only a small piece of bread and take only a sip or two of tea, and it was difficult for him to swallow even that much. Si Mokhtar would say to him: You get up earlier and work harder than I do. I'm much older than you are, and yet I eat twice as much as you. The farmer would look at him, shake his head and say: Your body's not like mine. It's strong. Mine isn't.

Si Mokhtar would ask him if he had sold everything and if everyone had paid cash, and the farmer would tell him what he had sold and bought, and how much money he had got and what he had paid out. They would go over each thing as they ate, and count the money that was left. After he had smoked three or four pipes of kif, Si Mokhtar would get up and go outside to pick pears. He put each pear carefully into a crate as he picked. When he grew tired of picking he would water the flowers and weed the vegetables for a while. After that he would wash his hands and feet, and go behind the fence to sit in his own spot between the kif patch and the tobacco patch. There he would smoke a few pipes and lie back and look up at the sky for a while, before he got up to go in and prepare his midday meal.

One day he went behind the fence to his spot. He sat down and began to smoke and drink tea, thinking about the world, and he looked at the kif growing beside him. It was a fine, light, silvery green. He looked at the tobacco and saw that it was very dark. Soon he leaned over and sniffed of the kif. It smelled sweet and fresh and spicy. And when he sniffed of the tobacco it had a rank odor. He turned to the kif: Yes, you're poison, he told it. If you catch a man you take a little of his blood right away. Then he looked at the tobacco and said to it: But you, your poison is really poison. When you catch a man you may not take his blood then, but a day can come when you'll take it all. He thought a while, and began to laugh. His laughter grew louder, and he looked up at the sky. But he was not crazy. He was thinking of the time that had not yet arrived in the world. The kif he was smoking made his thoughts shoot ahead, and he was able to see what was going to happen. Finally he spoke again. In the time that's coming, there's going to be fighting among men over both of you, he said to the kif and the tobacco. And he got up still laughing, and went out into the orchard to pull dead leaves off the plants. Soon he came to the clearing where nothing grew. He stood for a moment looking down at the ground, and he told it: I'm sorry. I can't give you water and I can't give you food. If I do, I'll lose the thing I love, the thing that makes me happy. I can't give you anything, because I want to stay this way always, with the same life I have now. When the good hour comes each evening I'm happy, and I live with my thoughts. He walked on slowly and watered his trees, and afterwards he went to wash. He ate his supper, made a pot of tea, and went to sit in the clearing. It was the good hour. He spread out his small sheepskin on the ground, set his pipe and his glass of tea on it, and one by one lighted all the carbide lamps that he had put around the clearing.

He sat down and waited. After a while the small slugs began to come out and move around. This was what Si Mokhtar loved more than everything else. The slugs were of many different colors, and they crawled this way and that, and touched each other, and went on. For Si Mokhtar they were always something very beautiful and very rare. Not many people can watch a thing like this every evening, the way I can, he thought. And he stayed very still, looking at them, for many hours, until he grew sleepy. Then he blew out all the lamps and went into his room and slept.

Not far away, above the valley where he lived, a French army officer had bought a piece of land and built a house on it. For a year or more Si Mokhtar saw the workmen come each day, and he was sad when the house was all finished and the Nazarenes came to live in it. Whenever the Frenchman and his wife had guests, they sat on the terrace in front of their house and looked down across Si Mokhtar's land. They could see the word ALLAH written out in Arabic letters by the plants in his garden, and the five-pointed star made by the flower-beds. They would look at the

11

shady orchard and the gardens down below, and then out at their own empty land where there were only cactuses and rock. They thought it was wrong that a Moslem should have all those trees and flowers when they had none. And at night, when Si Mokhtar lighted all the lamps around his clearing, the officer would look down from his window and see the lights flickering among the trees, and he would curse in anger. Sometimes he would see a man in a djellaba stand up and walk around for a moment, and then he would see him disappear as he sat down again. What's he doing down there? the Frenchman kept saying to himself.

One day at noon, when the sun was hot, Si Mokhtar stepped out into the clearing and saw one of the slugs lying alone on the bare ground. This had never happened before, and it astonished him. He bent down and whispered to it. Poor thing, what are you doing here? You'll die if you stay here in the sun, and you mustn't do that. You've got to go on living with your brothers. He shed a tear or two, took a leaf from a tree, and put the slug on the leaf. With the leaf in his hand he walked over to where there was some wet grass beside the well, and set the leaf down in the grass. All afternoon long he kept going to look at it, but it was still on the leaf. At twilight, when the slugs came out and began to move around, he picked up the leaf with the slug on it and carried it over to put it with the others. Then he went to prepare his evening tea. But that night as he sat watching the slugs he began to worry, and soon he bent over and said to them: Something's wrong. It's not the way it was. If I'd only known the Nazarene was going to buy that land, I'd have bought it myself, and he'd never have come to live so near us. It's too bad he got it before I found out. He was quiet for a while, and then he told them: That Nazarene is going to spoil the life we have together. He put his head to the ground and looked closely at his slugs for such a long time that he fell into a trance.

The officer was standing by his bedroom window in the dark, looking down at the lights that burned around Si Mokhtar's clearing. Each minute he felt more angry and nervous. Soon he told his wife that he was not coming to bed. He dressed and went out to the stables. There he got onto his horse and rode into the city to the barracks. He woke up four soldiers and told them they were going to ride with him to Boubana. When they got there he said: You go down there and see what that savage is doing, and come back here and tell me.

The four soldiers went down to Si Mokhtar's land and began to pound on the gate and call out. The dogs made a great noise with their barking. This brought Si Mokhtar out of his trance, and he was very angry. He jumped up and ran to unchain the dogs. Then he opened the gate. The two dogs rushed out like two bullets and attacked the soldiers. Two of the men fell, and the other two ran. When the two on the ground had been badly bitten, they scrambled to their feet and ran after the others towards the highway, firing four shots back at the dogs as they ran. The dogs stopped barking and went back to the orchard. Si Mokhtar chained them up again. He was still very angry.

He went into the house and came out with an axe. Then he ran out into the dark after the soldiers, and went on running until he got to the highway. When he saw them standing in front of the officer's house he shouted: What do you want of me? Where did you ever meet me? Why do you come in the middle of the night and disturb me? I don't want to know you or see you. This is my land, and I live here with my trees and my slugs.

The soldiers kept asking him what he was doing with all those lights burning, but they did not try to go near him. When he heard their questions, he began to swing the axe in the air. You want to know what's in there with the lights? he cried. What difference does it make to you what's there? Everything I have is there! My life is there! But you'll never get to see it!

He ran back to his house and put the axe away. In his bedroom he sat down trembling, smoked four pipes of kif, and fell asleep. When he awoke in the morning he was still trembling. He thought a moment. Then he went out to the clearing and began to spread dirt over the bare patch of ground, and on top of the dirt he poured water. He looked sadly at the clearing, and said to it: I've given you food and I've given you water.

When evening came he went to the place and looked. There was nothing moving. No slugs came out. He waited for a long time, but nothing happened. Then he knew everything was finished, and he began to sob. He blew out the lamps and went to bed.

In the morning he got up very early before the farmer had come, and walked all the way to the city. It was many years since he had been there, and the noise and confusion made him feel that he was about to explode. He rushed this way and that through the streets, sometimes running like a crazy man, until finally he found his way back to the road that led out to Boubana. When he got to his orchard he went in and walked behind the fence to the place between the kif and the tobacco. He let the two dogs loose so they could run around, and sat down to smoke. But his heart was beating very hard and his head was hot.

After his second pipe he began to feel very ill. I'm going to die, he thought. He could feel the dark growing inside his head, but in spite of that he sat up and began to write with his forefinger in the dirt beside him. *This is our land. If you are my brothers and you love me you will never sell it.*

And Si Mokhtar died then, just as he had expected. And the two dogs put their noses together and began to speak with each other. The black dog lay down beside Si Mokhtar, and the white one went running out of the orchard. He crossed the river and climbed up the side hill to the cemetery, and from there he ran on to Mstakhoche until he got to the house where Si Mokhtar's brother lived. There he barked and scratched at the door. When the man opened the door and saw the dog's eyes, he said to his wife: Mokhtar is dead. And he leapt onto his horse, and with the dog running behind, galloped down to Boubana. Si Mokhtar lay there, with the black dog lying beside him. He read the message written in the dirt, and he bent down and said to Si Mokhtar: I swear to you, *khai.* We'll never sell it.

BARAKA

SINCE BARAKA'S FATHER had two houses, he let Baraka live by himself in the empty one. It consisted of two ground-floor rooms and a kitchen and bathroom. The large room was fully furnished. Baraka preferred the small room, which had a mat, a taifor, a mattress and a wardrobe. On the taifor he kept a large bowl filled with a mixture of almonds, walnuts, honey and black jduq jmel seeds.

Afternoons Baraka would sit and brew a pot of tea. He would eat two spoonfuls of the mixture and drink two glasses of very hot tea. A little later he would smoke a kif cigarette.

This story is not one that can be proven, but it is certain that he would shut his eyes and lie back on the cushions with his head against the wall, and begin to dream. He always dreamed that he was wandering in an orchard. It was a strange place, like nowhere he had ever been before. Wherever he walked there were roses under the trees. Roses in all directions; he could walk a kilometer and never cease to see them.

Sometimes he would reach a place from where he could see, far ahead, faint glimpses of another orchard where the trees were taller, and it seemed to him that he could hear a great crying of birds in the distance. The day he managed to get to the second orchard, the sight of it made him stand motionless. He watched the birds as they circled above the trees. Finally he sat down, leaning against a tree trunk, and listened for a long time to the sound of the birds.

There were two of them in the tree above his head. Soon they

15

began to fly down and hover in front of his face without touching him. They would be there for an instant, and then they would dart up into the tree. For a long time they played this game with him. What do they want? he wondered. He got up, and the birds disappeared quickly into a hole in the tree-trunk.

That's strange, he said.

He stood for a while looking at the hole, and soon they came out and flew away. This was the moment to look into the hole. Inside was a nest with two featherless fledgelings in it.

Allah! he cried. I was going to kill those birds if they didn't stop their game, but they only wanted to get some food for their family.

At that moment his eyes opened. He stood up and went to the taifor, where he sat writing the entire story in a notebook. Then he went back and sat where he had been sitting before. He shut his eyes, took himself back to the orchard, and began to walk again.

After a while he came to a hillside covered with trees. There was a long path leading upward. He climbed slowly. When he got to the top he saw a field where many mongooses were running among the bushes. When they caught sight of him they all disappeared into their holes. He stood and watched, and saw their pointed muzzles appear in the openings, one by one. He sat down. Strange animals, each one in his hole. When I first saw them they were all out there playing together.

After a time he got up and walked toward the holes. The mongooses did not not pull their heads in, but stayed where they were, watching him. When he stooped over they all ran inside.

These animals understand, he said to himself. I'm going to keep looking. He sat down under a tree nearby and waited. Soon their heads appeared in the holes again, and they began to watch him.

Suddenly one of the mongooses came all the way out of its hole. I wonder why he came out?

As he said this the mongoose darted forward and seized a large snake that was crawling not far from where Baraka sat. Baraka jumped up, crying: *Ay yimma!* and ran to find a stick. By the time he got back the mongoose had bitten the snake's head off and was running away with it. Then the others came out of their holes and set to work eating the snake. When they had finished it, they went back to their holes.

Baraka opened his eyes. He got up, rolled himself a kif cigarette, and wrote down what he had pust seen. After a while he returned to the mattress and relaxed, in order to get back quickly to the orchard and see what would happen next.

He found the place where the mongooses had eaten the snake. I must go further, he thought, and see what's ahead. It can always be even better.

He cut across the hill, always walking among trees, and went downward to a river, whose course he followed until he came to a series of pools. The air was fresh and he could hear the river running nearby. He chose a pool and sat down beside it. As he looked into the water he saw two fish with brightly shining scales. He reached behind him, pulled up some plants, and tossed them into the water. The fish came up to the surface and nibbled at them.

Strange, he thought. Even fish eat weeds. Allah, what a garden! It's what all gardens should be. I can walk here, and yet no one has been here before me. What patterns the fish have on their scales! It would be a sin to eat such fish. They should be kept where people can see them.

It was a warm day. He reached out to feel the water with his finger. There was a sudden sharp pain, and he pulled back his hand. When he looked at the finger, he saw that half of it had been bitten away. With the blood running from his finger, he went in search of a plant with a yellow blossom. When he found one, he broke its stem. A milky liquid ran out, and he let it run onto his finger. It burned. He wound his handkerchief around the finger and went back to the pool. There were clots of blood in one part of the water. As he watched, another kind of fish appeared, silvery and flat, and sucked in the blood.

Strange, said Baraka. I never thought such a thing could happen.

It frightened him, and he decided these were not fish, after all. But what else could they be?

At that moment he opened his eyes. He was clutching his wounded finger, and the sweat ran down his cheeks. When he looked closely at his finger, he saw with relief that the flesh was all there. It was a dark purple color. He stood up and went over to the taifor. He found it painful to write, but he managed to put down everything that had happened. Then he went back to his seat and shut his eyes.

This time he passed the pools by the river and continued further. Soon he came to a forest of such huge trees that there was

17

only darkness beneath them. He was convinced that there was something even more important in here. He began to walk between the trees in the gloom, feeling his way among their trunks, and going very slowly. He continued ahead in this way for a while. Finally he saw a pale sliver of light beyond. When he got to the clearing, he realized that it would be impossible for him to go further, because the roots of the trees formed a high wall. They rose up sheer and wet, high above his head. He tried again and again to get a foothold, but he always slipped back. He walked first one way and then the other, and found only the wall of roots.

Then in the air above his head he heard a sound. A great bird was flying down upon him. As it came nearer, one of its wings hit him, and he fell headfirst to the ground, striking his forehead. He sat up, put his hand to his face, and felt the blood. Then he leaned back against a tree-trunk, feeling faint.

The bird had its nest nearby. It stayed a while there, and then it flew away. Baraka opened his eyes a little, and from where he lay, he looked around. He saw the nest and got up. There were three large eggs in it. Then he noticed that the eggs were moving. This frightened him, and he returned to the tree.

Soon he saw one of the small birds break through its shell. As he looked, the other two also hatched. Two of them were healthy, and the other was feeble.

The parents arrived. Baraka watched them feed the young birds. The two healthy ones ate hungrily, but the weak one would not touch the food. When the father saw this, he seized the weak one in his beak, and the pieces of broken shell in his claws, and flew away with them. Soon he returned, carrying nothing.

Baraka opened his eyes. He was sitting forward on his mattress, holding his forehead and sweating. He got up and went into the bathroom. There he stood in front of the mirror, looking to see if there was blood on his forehead. The pain where he had fallen was so strong that he expected to see a great amount of blood. However, there was only a drop.

He went back to his mattress saying: Strange. Such things don't happen. Wait while I fill a cigarette with kif.

He made the cigarette. While I smoke it I'll drink a glass of tea. And then back to my place to see what happens next.

He put the teapot onto the mijmah to heat. When it was ready he poured himself a glass of tea and lighted his cigarette. Afterward he shut his eyes. Quickly he was back in the darkness of the forest, near the wall of tree-roots. He found the nest, and looked at it as he passed. There was nothing in it.

And now he discovered a way of getting past the wall of roots, into the other part of the forest. It was a narrow winding passage. As he pushed ahead, he became aware of a red light flickering in the distance. He watched it moving, and knew it was fire. After a while he came to where he could see the flames. There was a cave ahead, and in its floor was a huge hole, full of fire. As he stood looking, there was an explosion, and the fire belched up like red water out of the hole, higher and higher, until the roof of the cave was a glowing crescent.

This sight delighted Baraka, for he felt that he had come upon something marvellous. He walked on through the maze of roots. The passage led him out onto open ground at the top of a steep cliff. Far below there was another forest, but he would have needed a two-hundred-yard rope to reach the bottom. He saw that if he went for miles along the edge of the cliff he might find a way down.

Baraka stood for a while, letting his eye run over the landscape. Then he turned and looked down at the earth near his feet. Not far away squatted a large spider, covered with black hairs. Its eyes were bright blue. As he watched, it began to move toward him. Fear seized him, and the skin tightened all over his body.

Baraka began to run, back into the maze of roots. Several times he looked over his shoulder and saw the spider coming along behind him. When he got to the darkest part of the forest he stopped looking back, and merely ran. It took him hours to get to the orchard where the roses grew. Then he turned again to see, but as he was looking back he ran full tilt into a tree. There was a terrible crash, and he opened his eyes.

He was sitting upright on his mattress, staring ahead of him. His breath came in gasps and his clothes were drenched with sweat. He looked at the table. The spider was there, on the edge of the bowl of jduq jmel paste. Now that he had made it real, he was no longer afraid of it. He thought: Other men dream and return with nothing. But I've learned how to bring things back. *Hamdoul'lah!*

THE SAINT BY ACCIDENT

THERE WAS A POOR MAN named Bouqoudja who had seven children. He was a *nchaioui* who smoked kif day and night. His habit was to go fishing at Achaqar on the Atlantic coast, at the place where there is a cave. Outside the entrance there is a hole in the rocks where the fishermen get fresh water.

One night when he was fishing Bouqoudja went to the hole to get some water, and he set down a large candle on the rocks. His head was full of kif, and after drinking he went away, leaving the candle burning. The following morning when he returned, it was still burning. He went into the cave and sat down in the dark.

A family arrived at Achaqar to spend the day on the beach, and they came upon the water-hole with the lighted candle beside it. Oh, an altar! they cried. Then they looked into cave and saw the man sitting in the darkness inside. He was smoking kif, but they did not notice that. They said nothing, in order not to disturb him, and went back to leave some coins beside the candle. These were for the saint who they thought was living in the cave. When Bouqoudja came out he saw the money. He put it into his pouch and went fishing.

That night he had good luck there at Achaqar. As he caught each fish, he tossed it up onto the rocks so that it fell near the water-hole beside the cave. The fish spattered drops of blood onto the rocks. At dawn he left the beach and went back to the town to sell the fish. He did the marketing for his family and went home.

What do you think? he said to his wife. And he told her how he had found the money by the water-hole. He decided to buy an oil lamp and put it there, instead of a candle.

When he returned to Achaqar, he discovered a hen with its throat cut, lying on the rocks. People had come and found the spots of blood there, and said to each other: Aha! They bring chickens here to sacrifice!

They began to carry fowl and kill them by the water-hole. Each time they came, they left money lying there on the rocks. Sometimes they left a whole chicken with its throat cut, or even a live one tied by its leg. There was so much to eat that Bouqoudja no longer fished. He began to wear a white turban. Then he bought a white djellaba and a white tchamir. And he let his beard grow long. He whitewashed the rocks all around the water-hole, and spent all his time in the cave.

One day a man and a woman came to see him. Sidi, they said, we have a son who is very sick. We'd like you to look at him, and write out some words for him.

Bouqoudja took a bottle and washed it thoroughly. He filled it with the water from the hole, and said to them: Give the child a spoonful of this three times a day. The people handed him a blessing of money and went away. At home they gave the boy the water as Bouqoudja had instructed. The boy got well, and they came back to see the saint.

Here's the boy. He's well. Hamdoullah! And now we want to give you a baraka.

He thanked them and they went away.

A khalifa who had heard of the shrine of Sidi Bouqoudja came to visit it, bringing his soldiers with him. They prepared a feast there on the rocks, and the khalifa went to the cave to talk with the saint.

Bouqoudja was sitting in the darkest part of the cave. The kif smoke was very strong.

What are you doing in here? demanded the khalifa, sniffing. Where's the saint?

Bouqoudja did not reply, and the khalifa went out of the cave, and left nothing on the rocks for the saint.

One night not long afterwards the khalifa was asleep. In his dream he saw the man who had been sitting in the cave, and the man looked at him sternly and said: Give me what is mine.

But what is yours? asked the khalifa.

The man did not reply.

21

The khalifa awoke with a start, and was not able to get to sleep again that night. The next day he decided to send some soldiers to Achaqar to fetch Sidi Bouqoudja.

When they brought Bouqoudja before him, the khalifa first begged his pardon. I didn't recognize you, he said. I'm going to give you what is yours.

And he handed Bouqoudja a great sum of money. Sidi Bouqoudja took it and said: Bismillah. The soldiers went back with him to the cave and left him.

Then Bouqoudja went to the town to see his wife. Allah has helped me, he told her. The khalifa has given me a fortune. Now we must move to Tetuan.

They went to Tetuan, where Bouqoudja bought an entire quarter containing twelve houses. He and his family moved into the largest one. The other eleven houses he rented to people with no money. If they were able to pay rent, he took it. If they could not, he let them stay anyway. And he often took them food. The money the khalifa had given him provided Bouqoudja's chance to become a true saint.

When sick people asked to be cured, he was able to help them with the words of Allah, because he was now a saint. To the people who came to see him he was much greater than any doctor. He used to say to them: Have faith, and you can sleep with snakes. And they still go to the water-hole, even though Sidi Bouqoudja has been dead for many years, and they light candles and leave food and money for him still.

ABDESLAM AND AMAR

WHEN ABDESLAM'S FATHER DIED, he left him his farm with its cows, sheep and goats. Most of the money he got for his milk and vegetables he brought back to his wife Zohra, and she hid it away for him. Some of it, however, he spent on kif, for he was a heavy smoker. He smoked in the café all day, and when he went home at night he continued to smoke. Zohra would sit beside him on the mattress, and as he smoked he would invent long stories to amuse her.

One night Abdeslam came home with his head more full of kif than usual. He went to sleep without telling any stories. During the night Zohra began to shake him. Wake up! she cried. The sick cow is dying. Kill her now, before she dies, or no one will be able to eat the meat. If you get there in time we can use it or sell it. Get up!

Abdeslam got up and tok a long knife with him out to the stable. It was dark there, and the kif in his head sent him to the mule's stall. He cut the mule's throat according to ritual, and went back to bed. I killed her, he told Zohra. Tomorrow morning early I'll skin her.

It was Zohra who got up first. When she went to the stable she found that the cow had died. Then she saw the mule with its throat cut. She ran to Abdeslam. Now we've got no meat and no mule either.

Abdeslam sprang up and went to look. Allah! he cried. How am I going to get back and forth to the city?

Zohra comforted him. You've got plenty of money, she told him. Why don't you take some of it and go to a souk and buy a horse?

And ride it back. Or buy a mare too, and they might have a colt.

You're right, I suppose, he said. But I'll have to go today.

She brought him a pile of money and wrapped it in a big hand-kerchief. Then Abdeslam set out on foot. It was summer, and the countryside was very hot. When he came to a stream he sat down in the shade of the trees on the bank. After he had rested a while he pulled out his kif pipe and smoked a little. Presently he said to himself: I'm going to take my clothes off and bathe in the river.

He laid his pipe, his mottoui and his matches under some bushes by the trunk of a tree. And he undressed, leaving his clothing on the ground, with the handkerchief full of money on top. Then he walked toward the water.

At that moment a large dark bird flew down. He turned, and seeing it perched on top of his clothing, began to run back. The bird flapped away as he approached, with the bundle of money hanging from its claws. It did not go very fast, and it flew over the trees. Abdeslam ran after it, naked as he was, and followed its shadow as it flew. Soon he was out of breath, and dropped to the ground. From there he watched the bird as if flew further and further away and disappeared.

A Riffian named Amar was making a pilgrimage to the tomb of Sidi Bouchaib, which was in that region. Already he had passed through thirty villages, and he had only five more to go through before he reached the tomb. As he wandered along the banks of the stream, he came upon the pile of clothing left there by Abdeslam. He began to call out, to see if their owner was nearby. No answer came, and there was no one in sight. Then he took off the rags he wore and threw them into the stream. He dressed in Abdeslam's clothing and went on his way. After he had passed through three more villages he was tired, and he sat down beside a spring that bubbled out of the rocks.

After watching the bird disappear with his money, Abdeslam rested a while on the ground. Then he rose and went back to where he had left his clothing by the stream. He searched for a long time, but was unable to find anything. All he found were his pipe, his mottoui and his matches, which were under the bushes where he had left them. He sat down, still naked, leaning against the tree-trunk, and smoked a few pipes. Finally he began to say: No mule, no cow, no money, no clothes. No mule, no cow, no money, no clothes.

When night came and it grew late, he got up and walked home.

He met no one on the way.

Zohra cried out when she saw him come in naked. Allah! What has happened?

He raised his arms and looked at her. No mule, no cow, no money, no clothes, he told her. Then he collapsed on the mattress.

What's the matter? she cried.

I'm dying, said Abdeslam. My heart is pounding.

She heated water and washed him and put his tchamir on him. Then she made him sit up and take the soup she had prepared for him. Later she served him dinner. He ate heavily, and then he started to smoke kif. Finally he went to bed.

Amar the pilgrim slept all night beside the spring. In the morning he drank all the water he could hold, and set out again. It was a very hot day, and he soon grew thirsty. When he came to a grove of trees, he walked in, looking for water. As he went along he came upon an open space near a stream. A large bird stood there, eating something it had caught. Nearby on a rock lay a white bundle, carefully wrapped and tied, but there was not a person in sight.

Amar began to walk toward the bundle. As he got to it, the bird came flying at him, and attacked him with its beak. All the clothing he had found the day before was slashed into strips, and the skin on his body was cut open.

Finally the idea came to him that he must bite off the bird's head. Even when he had done this, his rage continued, and he ripped out the bird's feathers. And he disembowelled it. He washed the carcass in the stream, made a fire, and roasted it over the flames.

When he had eaten the bird and smoked a few pipes of kif, he decided to look at the bundle. He untied it and stared at the money. Then, feeling very happy, he tied it all up again and continued to walk until he got to the saint's tomb.

There he went inside and left a little money beside the shrine. He resumed his journey through the country, stopping to rest in a small village at the end of each day. When he came to a large town he decided to buy new clothes. The bird had clawed the others into rags. This time he had all his garments made of felt, so that when he was dressed in them he looked like a khalifa. He bought a magnificent white horse and a fine saddle, and started out for the Rif.

At the fourth village he went to a café and bought some kif, which he prepared and cut. In that village they aged their kif, and their tobacco was fiery, the best. He made a cutting of kif that was kif and a half, and packed it into his mottoui.

He got onto his white horse again and rode on, until he came to the village where Abdeslam lived. And he rode through the street, looking like a pacha or a vizir, and Abdeslam was walking along in the dust. He saw the horse, and paused to admire it as it went past. Then he looked up at the rider and said: *Salaam aleikoum.*

Aleikoum salaam, replied Amar.

You're a stranger here, said Abdeslam.

Yes. I come from a long way off. From here to my tchar it's thirty villages.

Welcome to our tchar, Abdeslam told him. Where are you going now?

I'm looking for a café.

Come with me. I'll take you to a good place.

Amar dismounted. They walked to the café, where he tied his horse at the entrance.

That's a fine horse, said Abdeslam. Do you want to sell him?

No, no. I can't sell him, Amar said.

Abdeslam laughed. Whatever can't be sold is a sin, you know, he said. Amar smiled, and they went into the café.

They ordered two glasses of tea. Amar took out his pipe and his mottoui. Seeing this, Abdeslam did the same. Each one smoked his own kif, and neither one offered his to the other. Two friends of Abdeslam's came into the café and sat down with them. They also took out their pipes and mottouis, and the four smoked a while, talking.

Then Amar said he must be on his way. He paid for the teas. Abdeslam got up, and they went out.

As they stood in front of the café, Abdeslam turned to Amar and said: Why don't you come home and eat with me and spend the night? And in the morning if you want to go on, you can go.

Amar thanked him, and they went to the house. Zohra brought in the taifor with the dinner on it. Afterward they drank tea. Then Abdeslam, feeling happy after his meal, said to Amar: Here. Fill your pipe from my mottoui. And Amar then had to say to Abdeslam: Yes. Fill yours from mine.

I think you'll find mine better, said Abdeslam. It's very good.

Amar replied: That's what I think about mine.

26

Abdeslam waited a moment, and then he said: My kif is going to make you dizzy. I warn you.

Mine may kill you, Amar told him, and they both laughed.

Abdeslam handed Amar his pipe, already lighted, saying: Here. Smoke my kif. And see what it'll do to you.

Amar took the pipe and smoked it, and blew out the ball of ash.

Your kif didn't even reach the veins in my temples, he told Abdeslam. I'm going to fill the pipe for you with my kif.

He filled the pipe and handed it to Abdeslam. Pull on it hard and swallow all the smoke, he told him.

Abdeslam took a hard pull at the pipe and inhaled. Then he kept the smoke in his lungs. His eyes started from his head, and tears spouted from them. He could not breathe. He fell to the floor, and the sweat came out on his face. He was dead. Amar did not spend the night there.

In the morning the house was filled with Zohra's cries. The fqih came and chanted over the dead man. They carried him to the cemetery and buried him. Forty days later Amar returned to the village and married Zohra.

WHAT HAPPENED IN GRANADA

I USED TO WORK for an American in Tangier, driving his car for him. His wife often had to go and stay for a while in the hospital in Spain. One day the American said to me: I've got to take Mrs. James back to the hospital. If only you hadn't let your passport expire, you could come. While I'm over there you ought to go and try to get a new one.

Yes, I said, I will.

He took his wife to Malaga and left her in the hospital there. By the time he got back to Tangier I had my passport. A few months later he went to see her. He wanted me to go with him, but I was feeling sick. At the hospital the doctor told him that his wife was much better and could leave at any time. She was not really well, but he decided to take her up to Granada, where there was an English family he knew. They had a large house and were willing to let her stay with them if he paid for her room and food. He explained to them that he could not take her home because every time she got to Tangier she fell sick again. He left his wife with them, and came back to Tangier.

A few days later the telephone rang. One of the English women was saying that he must come right away to Granada and get his wife. We can't take care of her, she said. We can't have her in the house. And you knew very well we couldn't have her. You come here and get her. We're very angry with you, and we'll talk to you when you get here.

Mr. James tried to say: How is my wife? But the English woman had hung up. He did not understand what had happened.

Will you come with me this time? he asked me, and I said yes, I would go with him.

We left on a Tuesday, and got to Malaga that night. The next morning we were up early. Mr. James wanted to go to the hospital and see if they had an empty room for his wife. The doctor said there was one, and that he could bring her back if he liked. We went to an agency that rented cars and asked them what they had. There were only three cars: a Séat, a Simca and a Renault. I went outside to look at them, and chose the Séat. As we went back into the office the telephone rang and the girl answered it.

The Séat is rented, she said when she came over to the counter. I just rented it. And she pointed to the telephone. I was angry, but I was a foreigner there and couldn't say anything. So now which one do you want? she asked me.

I'll take the Renault, I said. We paid and took the car's papers. First we drove to a restaurant and had lunch. Then we went to the hotel and paid the bill and put the luggage into the car.

We started out. Halfway up into the mountains the brakes started slipping. I did not want to say anything about it to Mr. James because he might worry. It was very hot and sunny. When we got to Granada the air was full of dust. We found our way up to the Albaicin. I parked and we got out. We knocked on the door. A girl opened it. She was about seventeen and had blond hair. She told us to come in, and was sat down in the bar.

Mr. James asked if he could see the girl's aunt. She did not answer, and so he said: How is Mrs. James?

What will you have to drink? she asked him. Beer or whiskey?

I'd like to see your aunt, he told her.

She looked at me. And you? she said. Won't you have something? Some beer?

I don't drink, I said. I'll take a glass of water.

She brought a glass of water for me and a Coca Cola for Mr. James. We sat down and drank, and then he started up the stairs to see his wife. I went up behind him. The two English women were with her in her room. We went in and she kissed her husband first. Then she kissed me. I saw the two English women look at each other and I knew they hated all three of us.

We went downstairs and out into the garden, the Americans and the two English women and I. Mr. James began to talk with his wife. He wanted to know how she felt, and whether she liked the place where she had been staying. After a while I got up and began to pull dead leaves out of the flower pots. Everything was falling to pieces and covered with dust.

One of the women came over to where I stood and said: That's nice of you. We haven't had time to make any repairs. We just bought the house a little while ago. Come. I want to show you the garden in the patio. Do you like plants? We were climbing up the steps to go into the patio.

It's my work, I said. Every kind of plant. That's a big garden there, and you have a fine view from it.

That building you saw over there on the other side of the valley belonged to the Moslems once. She looked at me. Are you their chauffeur?

Yes, I said.

Where are you from?

From the Rif.

The Riffians are good people, she said. We looked at the flowers, and then she went up the stairs that led to the gallery, and I went back to the garden and sat down with the Americans. After a while the husband of one of the English women came into the garden. He was a heavy bald man with a little pointed beard. He was carrying an open book in front of him, looking down at it as he walked. He offered me a cigarette and I took it. The first thing he said to me was: What part of the Rif are you from?

I'm from Temsaman.

That's a fine country, he said. I've lived for a long time in the Rif, and seen some of Temsaman.

I was surprised to hear that. You have? I said.

I speak a little Riffian.

His wife came out then. What will you have to drink? she asked me.

I said I didn't want anything. She brought me Coca Cola. The Englishman went to the bar to put more whiskey into his glass. His wife was telling the Americans about a doctor she knew. She said his office was not far, and she would take them to see him, because he might give Mrs. James some medicine to make her sleep.

A little later we started out. I helped Mrs. James walk to the car, with my arm around her, and I put her in front with me. Mr. James and the English woman sat in the back. The streets were narrow and there were holes in the pavement. Finally we arrived at the doctor's office. I had an empty bottle of vitamins in my pocket, and I wanted to buy another like it.

I found a pharmacy and asked for the pills. They looked, and came back and said they did not have them. All right, I said. Give me two cans of talcum powder. As he handed me the change I saw him staring at my feet, because I was wearing Moroccan *belrha*. I carried the parcel to the car and locked it in. Then I went back into the waiting-room and spoke to Mr. James.

Still waiting?

That's right.

I'm going out and get a cup of coffee, I told him.

As I walked along the street all the Spaniards looked at me. I went into a café and said: *Buenas tardes* to the men inside, but nobody answered. They only frowned at me. I asked for a *café con leche*.

The man brought a cup of something that a dog wouldn't have taken. How much? I asked him.

Three pesetas.

I held up the coffee and poured it out so that it fell near my feet. Then I pulled out ten pesetas and tossed them over the counter onto the floor. The man leaned over, picked up the money and put it into his pocket. I stood in the doorway, looked at everybody in the café, and laughed. I decided to go back to the doctor's office.

You're still here?

Still waiting.

I took a chair from the waiting-room and carried it outside to the street, where I put it in front of the door. Then I sat watching the people walk by. Beside me there was a glass table with a pot of flowers on it. In the corner stood two big pots with palms in them. On the front of the building there were several colored pictures of Jesus Christ, made of tiles.

After a while I got up and went inside again. The English woman began to ask me questions.

Where were you born?

Who? Me?

Yes. You.

In the Rif.

Which part?

I was born in Temsaman.

I've heard it's a nice place, she said.

31

It's good to people who are good to it, I told her. She looked at me.

But it's not so good for the others.

She sniffed. All Riffians are like that, she said.

Yes. You have to treat them carefully. A lot of people don't understand them, so they say they're no good.

My husband and I lived in the Rif. We liked the people. They're very different from city people, she said.

City people are modern, but the Riffians are strong. They have another life, a different world.

Suddenly she said: What do you think about the trouble in Israel? What about Egypt and Jordan? Why don't they get together and finish off Israel?

That's none of my business, I said. I don't understand anything about those things.

Then she said: I heard on the BBC that Egypt is going to let the Jews stay in Israel.

If Egypt lets the Jews stay in Israel, Franco will have to let the Moroccans have Andalucia, I told her.

She stopped talking. What's the matter? I asked her.

Nothing, she said quickly, and shut her mouth. At that moment the doctor came out, and all three of the Nazarenes went with him into his office.

I walked out into the street, and went into a small store nearby to buy a bar of chocolate. Then I sat in the Renault and ate half the bar. Mr. James came out of the office with his wife and the English woman, and they got into the car. As we were driving through the Albaicín on our way up to the house, a Spanish boy on a bicycle who was playing with some others steered it right in front of us. When he saw the car so near to him, he was frightened and fell off the bicycle. I had to put on the brakes very hard.

Why don't you look where you're going? I asked him.

And who are you? he cried.

I got out of the car. If I'd killed you it would have been my fault, I told him. And why don't you show a little respect? Don't try to look so tough.

A man came up. Why are you talking to the boy? he demanded.

You saw what happened, I told him. And what difference does it make to you if I talk to him?

He's a relative of mine.

32

Then two more arrived. The English woman jumped out of the back of the car, got in front, slammed the door, and drove off, up the hill.

In another minute I was in the middle of thirty Spaniards, all talking at once. I yelled at them: I shit on your ancestors and your whole race! I kept walking along, pushing through them. Barking dogs don't bite, I told them. A very fat woman came by. She called me a *moro*, and I called her a Christian pig. There was a man without legs, sitting in a wheel-chair on the sidewalk. He called me a dirty moro, and I said: *Gracias*. I don't like to insult people without legs. You're the champion. You win.

I got up to the house, and went in through the patio and out into the garden. I sat down near the Englishman, who was in a chair under a tree, reading.

What happened? he wanted to know.

Nothing. I was talking to some Spaniards.

Have something to drink, he told me. I ordered a Coca Cola, and he offered me a cigarette.

I'd like to talk to you, he said. About you and about the Rif.

Why? I mean, I want to know why you want to know about me.

I just want to ask about some things I don't know, he said.

I see. You're writing a book, and you need to know those things before you can finish it. Is that right?

No.

I can't tell you anything, I said. You see, I'm writing a book about the Rif myself. I need to know some things too before I can finish mine.

I'm not writing a book, said the Englishman. And I'm not trying to find out any secrets. I only want to know what the Temsaman country is like. What have they got there, and what do they do?

What would they have? They have just what everybody else has.

And their saints? Sidi Bouchaib?

Yes, I said.

The hundred and one saints?

Yes.

He had drunk a lot of whiskey, but when his wife called to him from the bar he heard her. He got up and walked away.

Mr. James and his wife were upstairs. I smoked several cigarettes. Finally I stood up and began to walk around the garden, pulling off the dead leaves.

33

The sister of the English woman came out and saw me. Do you like plants? she asked.

I like them, and I feel sorry for these, I told her. They don't get any care.

We take care of everything, she said. We give all the plants water regularly.

Of course. But that's not enough. You have to loosen the soil around them and keep it loose. You can't just pour water on.

Yes, yes. We're going to get around to all that, she said. We'll take care of everything little by little. We have no money. We've got to make some money from that bar before we can paint the house and arrange the garden. There are many things we haven't done yet. Later.

Of course you need money to paint, I said. But it doesn't take money to keep plants healthy.

I know. But we'd have to have a gardener. Excuse me, she said, and walked away.

It was just half past eight, and I was getting hungry. One of the English women was with Mrs. James, and the other was with Mr. James, and they were both talking about me, telling them that I was the bad kind of Riffian, the kind that always looks for trouble wherever he goes. I walked up and down in the hallway outside the two rooms and heard them talking. Finally I was so hungry I went down to the bar where the girl was serving drinks to some Spanish people who had come in from the street.

Can you give me six skewers of meat, please? I said.

She went out and came back with one skewer. That's all we have, she told me.

After a while they all went into the dining-room upstairs, and Mrs. James saw that the table was laid for six people instead of seven.

Haven't you laid a place for our driver? she said.

Why doesn't he eat downstairs? said the English woman. He'd be happier there.

No, no! He always eats with us.

The English woman came down into the bar and said: Come upstairs.

I went up and sat with the Nazarenes. The servants brought the soup and I did not take any. The main course was chicken with potatoes. I turned my plate upside down. I did not want to eat because

34

I was afraid. They had a black cook from Marrakech. When I had first seen her, my heart had tried to escape from her. I did not trust her at all.

Mrs. James kept saying to me: You must eat. Why aren't you eating?

I don't want anything.

The English woman said: Oh, so you don't want to eat? Why not?

My stomach hurts. Besides, I had a pinchito downstairs, and it filled me up.

She did not say anything. The meal was not a meal. The servant brought the fruit. Two pieces of melon and four cherries for each person. And they looked as if they had been waiting for a month in the icebox.

When the Nazarenes had finished eating, they began to smoke cigarettes. A small boy came in. He was the son of the cook. Do you want coffee? he asked me in Arabic. A little coffee, and lots of milk, I said.

After I had drunk my coffee, Mr. and Mrs. James and I went out into the garden. We sat down around a table and looked across at the Moroccan palace on the other side of the valley. They had spotlights turned on it so it would look like a postcard. We could see all the lights of Granada below. The day had been very hot, but the night was cool. Mr. James and his wife were talking together, and I was thinking only of those four English people in the house, the man and his wife, and the sister with her daughter. I could see that they had a terrible life there.

In a little while some drunken Spaniards came out into the garden. One of them leaned against the wall, and a woman came and put her arms around his neck and began to kiss him. Then they would talk, and then kiss some more. This went on for nearly an hour.

Later the two English women came out. We were wondering where you were, they said, looking at Mr. James, and I could see that they had just been talking about him. Then they went back into the house. A friend of the two who were kissing came and took them into the bar. I was thinking that the English women were crazy. On the telephone they had said they were very angry, but when Mr. James was there with them they talked and joked with him as if they were his friends.

I'm sleepy, I told Mr. and Mrs. James. I'm going to bed. I went upstairs to the room where they had put me. It had a sewing-machine in it, and there were piles of old sheets and towels lying around. I had to go through Mr. James's room to get into it. I pulled the spread off the bed the woman had told me was mine. There was a dirty blanket under the spread, and no sheets. The mattress was very old and filthy. Then I looked at the second bed. It had one sheet. I lay down on the bed they had given me, but I could not sleep. The room was over the bar, and there was flamenco noise and loud dancing going on. I lay on one side and the other, and on my back, and people cried:*Olé!* and all the time I was wondering if I would ever get to sleep.

A little later I heard footsteps, and someone opened the door of my room. I saw the Englishman's wife come in. She was holding one hand behind her. She's got a knife, I said to myself, and she's coming to use it on me. She walked toward my bed, and I was getting ready for her. Then I saw her other hand. There was nothing in it. But she kept coming, until she was beside the bed. Then she bent over and picked up a roll of electric cord that was lying on the floor. I decided that she was going to pass the wire behind my head and try to strangle me with it. I reached out and pushed away the hand that was holding the wire. She was startled. It's all right. It's all right, she said. Go to sleep.

She carried the wire with her out of the room and shut the door. I sat up and smoked a cigarette. The noise down in the bar went on and on. No matter what I did, I couldn't fall asleep.

Finally the people left and they shut the bar. It was quiet for a few minutes. Then I heard a very loud bang, and voices in Mr. James's room. I jumped out of bed, and opened the door. I found the two English women, both very drunk, standing over Mr. James's bed, yelling at him. He had bolted his door, and between them they had broken it open.

Mr. James was sitting on his bed in his pyjamas with his head in his hands. Get up! they were saying. We're ready to talk to you now. He looked at his watch. But it's after three, he said. I want to sleep.

Ah, you want to sleep! They began to laugh very loud. But you're not going to sleep! You think you can just lock your door and go to bed? Put your clothes on, and come outside. We want to talk to you.

Get out of here, you Riffian! Go back into your room and shut

36

the door! cried the mother of the girl.

I looked her up and down, and said: A whole family of whores. If you weren't whores you wouldn't break into a man's room and stand over his bed and scream at him. Only whores do that.

The two women ran out of the room. Mr. James was putting on his clothes. When he was dressed, he went to his wife's room. She had heard all the noise and shouting, and was calling out to him.

I stood in the corridor, and when Mr. and Mrs. James came out of her room, we all went into the dining-room, where the two women stood with glasses of gin in their hands. Their eyes were very narrow. They began to tell Mr. James that they understood what he was doing, and that he was trying to make his wife sicker than she was, because he wanted to get rid of her. He would not speak to them. He only shrugged his shoulders.

I know what you want, I told them. I told Mr. James when we were on the boat. Those people want money, I said. Even before I've seen those English people I don't like them.

The Englishman's wife came over to me and said slowly: *Hijo de puta.* Then she slapped me, trying to hit my cheek, but I ducked, and she hit my neck. I punched her in the face with the back of my hand. She fell against the door and came back to hit me again. Then I slapped her hard with my left hand, and she went onto the floor. I lifted her up and pushed her against the table. The dishes broke and fell on the rug. By that time I was angry. There was an Arab sword hanging on the wall. I yanked it down.

I'm going to finish you off, you and your race! I told her. We'll all go to jail tonight except you. You're only an English whore and I'm a Riffian!

The woman's sister screamed and ran into the lavatory. She shut the door and bolted it, and began to pound on it with her shoe, screaming all the time. The Englishman's wife ran into the kitchen. I ran after her, trying to chop the top of her head with the sword. Then Mrs. James came up to me and took the sword out of my hand.

I went to my room and threw my clothes into my suitcase. I heard the English woman calling: Rifi! Rifi! If you're a Riffian, speak Riffian! What kind of Riffian are you?

When I came out into the corridor I saw her at the other end, peeking around the corner. I'm a Riffian! I shouted. What are you? An English Jewess, that's what you are. That's nothing much.

Jewess! she screamed. I'm not Jewish! I'm English!

The girl came up the stairs. The banging in the lavatory went on, and she could hear her mother shouting: Help! Help! The girl stood a minute, and then went and told her mother to come out. The woman cried and laughed, and her face was very white. At the same time the Englishman came downstairs reading a book. I stood with my valise in my hand, and looked at his head. It was like a watermelon, and his nose was like a rhaita. His wife said to him: Here he is! Speak to him in Riffian and see!

He loked over his glasses at me and said: *Mismiuren? Mismiuren* means: What's going on? But I did not want to speak Riffian.

I don't understand what you're saying, I told him.

He hung his head, and his wife cried: You see? He's not a Riffian.

I'm not like your husband, I told her. I haven't eaten donkey's ears. Look at him. He can't even lift his head. Any other man, when he hears his wife insulting somebody, speaks to her and makes her stop.

The woman began to shout: *Mierda! Mierda!*

I spit at her three times. She only shouted at her husband: Why don't you speak to him in Riffian?

I said to him: Yes. And why don't you speák to her in Hebrew? You need a lot more time if you want to learn Riffian. You think you know something about the Riffians? All you ever saw of them was their teeth when they smiled at you. They never let you find out the important things.

I went into Mrs. James's room and helped her pack her bags. I squeezed them all shut, and then I went to help Mr. James. When all their luggage was in the corridor, the girl came upstairs and told me: Wait. I'll turn on the light. I carried everything down and put it into the car, started the motor, and drove around to the front door. It was half past four in the morning, but I began to blow the horn, over and over. The Spaniards leaned out of their windows to watch. I looked at the house and said: *Inaal din d'babakum.*

Mr. James came down with his wife. I helped her into the front, and he got into the back. I shut the car door and spat at the house. Then I drove off.

I was very nervous going through Granada, and Mr. and Mrs. James were afraid of an accident, because they saw how I felt. We drove out of the city, went a few kilometers, and stopped for gasoline. It was still dark.

38

Mr. James got out while the Spaniard filled the tank. Then I asked for some water. He gave me a clay jar to drink from. The water was cold and sweet.

We went on our way. I was driving slowly, the way they liked me to drive. It began to get light. This is a good trip, I told them. It's cool and there are trees everywhere, and the wind smells good, and you can see the mountains far away. It's a good place to be driving through.

They both said I was right.

We came to a village and stopped. There was a café that was open. We all went in. Mr. and Mrs. James were very tired, and they sat down at a table near the door. I went and ordered a *café con leche* and a pastry for each of us. I started with a glass of orange juice, and Mrs. James gave me her pastry. We talked about the English people. Mr. and Mrs. James both said I had been right, but Mrs. James told me: I thank Allah you didn't manage to hit the woman's head with the sword.

Then we started to drive again, still very slowly. We were all so sleepy that our eyes were ready to shut. The road was nothing but curves. When we got to the mountains above Malaga it was full of trucks coming up and going down. A dangerous road. The foot brakes were not working at all, but we got to Malaga and went to the hotel. It was not yet seven o'clock.

We carried the luggage into the hotel, took three rooms, and went to bed. At noon we had to get up to go and see the doctor. I was up at eleven thirty, and I called Mr. and Mrs. James. We had some coffee and went out.

At the doctor's office Mr. and Mrs. James sat down to wait, and I went to look for the agency to return the car. I couldn't find it, no matter which street I took. Finally I parked the car and went to ask a policeman. He explained where the place was. I walked there, and told them they would have to go with me to get the car. A Spaniard went out with me, and we walked to where I had parked the car. He drove it back to the agency. On the way at a cross-street he put on the brakes. We kept going, so that he hit another car. I began to laugh, because he had found it out himself. When we got to the agency he went in and scolded the girl. Why do you go on giving cars to people without checking on the brakes? They might have had an accident.

It was lucky the car had a good driver, I told him.

He gave me the change and apologized. I went back to the doctor's office. They were talking with him. When they finished we all got into the elevator, and a nurse came along with us. We managed to get a taxi at the door, and drove to the hospital. It was outside the city in an orchard. Some nuns led Mrs. James away, and Mr. James stood talking to the Mother.

When Mr. James and I got to the port in Tangier, the sun was very hot and there was a strong wind blowing. He said he was glad to be on the other side of the water from the women in Granada. We passed through the customs and I drove him home.

THE WITCH OF BOUIBA DEL HALLOUF

There was a young man named Qaqo who lived in Tchar ej Jdid with his mother. The woman spent her days gathering wood in the forest. She would load it on her back and take it to the town, where she sold it to the bakers for their ovens. While his mother was in the forest looking for wood, Qaqo stood near a café selling pastries for a peseta apiece. If there were any left over at night, he would get up at six o'clock the next morning and sit in the doorway of the café, and the men who were having breakfast there would buy them all. Then he would go home and make fresh pastries. He took them to the oven to have them baked, and when they were done he would pile them on a tray and go to stand outside the café. By the time he got home his mother would have sold her wood and be in the house cooking dinner.

One evening when Qaqo got home she was not there. He waited a long time for her, and when she did not come, he started out to look for her. He climbed up the mountain to Sidi Amar, then by Rmilats and Donabo, and from there to Ain del Ouis and the entrance to Mediouna, and up to Bouiba del Hallouf, at the highest part of the mountain.

In the moonlight there on the trail he saw something dark. Then he heard a voice crying: Ay yimma! Ay yimma! and he knew it was his mother lying on the ground.

What's the matter?

I'm sick! she said. And nobody came by to help me.

He unstrapped her from the pile of wood, lifted her up, and carried her on his back until he got to the highway. There some

41

strangers passing by in a car helped him get her back to Tchar ej Jdid.

Qaqo put his mother to bed and made her a little harira. After she had drunk it, she fell asleep. And he spent the whole night sitting beside her and wondering.

In the morning she awoke, and saw Qaqo sitting there.

How do you feel? he asked her.

A little better, son.

Shall we eat? I've got everything ready. He brought her a bowl of harira, and mint tea with bread and honey. He watched her happily while she ate and drank. Then he said to her: Tell me all about it. What happened yesterday?

Yes, son, I'll tell you. Yesterday I didn't go where I usually go to look for the wood. I climbed down by the ocean and found a new place where there was wood everywhere. But there was a big hole in the ground near it, and when I looked down in I saw piles of bones. I went on as fast as I could and turned to the left, and I came to two big boulders, and the top of the mountain was above my head, very high, and the rocks went straight down to the sea on the other side. I went nearer, and between the two boulders there was an old woman with long white hair. She called to me, so I stopped. Then she came out, and I ran back. And she came running after me. I got out of the forest and ran toward the little farm up the road. There were two dogs, and they came out and began to bark. I turned around, and I saw her going back into the woods. Then I felt very sick, and walked around, and fell down. And it wasn't a woman that came after me, either. It was an affrita.

Qaqo began to laugh. Mother, he said. There are no affarits any more. The old woman is probably hiding there from the government, and she's got friends with her, smugglers perhaps. I'd like to see her myself. I'm going up and look for her.

No! Don't go there, please! I'll go crazy waiting for you to come back. They could kill you. And if anything happens to you I'll die.

Don't you think about it, Mother, he said. It's seven o'clock. I've got to go to work now and get rid of these pastries. There aren't many left.

Qaqo went out with only about twenty pastries on his tray. He sold them quickly to the men having their breakfast at the café. Then he bought enough kif to fill his mottoui, went to the market for food, and carried it home.

You can make lunch for yourself, he told his mother. Because I won't be here. I'll be back for dinner.

She knew where he was going. Be very careful, son. If they ever catch you they'll kill you.

Don't worry, said Qaqo.

He walked to Dradeb and then up the Monte Viejo. He cut through to the highway by the Palace of Moulay Abd el Aziz, and then followed along to Sidi Amar. He climbed up to the top of the great rock of Sidi Amar. The sun was warm. He sat down, looked at the mountains, and smoked many pipes of kif. Then he lay on his back and looked at the trees and the sky.

After a while he put away his pipe, climbed down the rock, and started walking again, straight to Bouiba del Hallouf. He stood on top of the cliff and looked at the big forest all around below him. The sight of it chilled him at first. But then he started down through the forest, taking the path his mother had described to him. It was not long before he came to the large hole in the ground. He peered in and saw the white bones far below. Then he went on, made the turn to the left, and soon came to the place of the two boulders. He stood still and listened. Then between the trees he saw a clearing where thousands of butterflies were trembling in the sunlight. The ground was covered with them, and they moved in the air under the trees. He went on into the forest. Again he stopped to listen and to smoke some kif, and now it seemed as though he could hear a woman's voice saying to him: Don't go on. Something will happen.

He looked upward, into the branches of a tree above him, and thought he could make out the face of an old woman caught in the thick spiderwebs that hung between the boughs.

Qaqo continued to walk ahead. Suddenly a girl stepped out from behind a tree and walked toward him. When she came up to him she stopped and said: Ahilan! How are you?

And you, he said. How are you?

I'm wondering what you're doing here, she told him.

Just looking at the forest. There's not another like it. I've been to many places, and we have the best one here at Bouiba del Hallouf.

Yes, you're right, she said. Come with me if you want to see more.

They started to walk together. Soon they came to the entrance to a large cave. Qaqo followed the girl inside, and they descended a

43

flight of stairs into a lower cave. There were trickles of water running down the walls of rock. The water ran into a trough that led to a pool below. When they got to the bottom of the steps, Qaqo saw that the pool was full of fish. There were many torches burning in this part of the cave.

Wait for me here. I'm going to change my clothes, the girl told him. I'll be right back.

Qaqo stood smoking kif by the edge of the pool while he waited. He was not certain whether what he was seeing was real or not because he had already smoked so much kif on the rock at Sidi Amar. Soon the girl arrived looking even more beautiful in a blue and gold kaftan.

What would you like to see? she asked him as they went back up the stairs.

You have butterflies, said Qaqo. I'd like to see them.

Don't you want to see what I have here in the cave? she said.

I want to see the butterflies first, he told her.

They walked out of the cave and through the forest to the clearing. As they stood there looking at the butterflies, again it seemed to Qaqo that he could hear a woman's voice. But this time it was laughing. He glanced up. There was something that looked like the face of a very old woman wrapped in the spiderwebs between the branches. Her mouth seemed to be saying: Look out! Be careful!

The girl was shivering as she looked at the butterflies lighting and fluttering their wings. I hate those things! she cried.

Then Qaqo gave her a powerful push, so that she fell onto the earth among the butterflies. He could scarcely see her, there were so many of them around her. She began to scream, and as she screamed she started to look like the thing he had just seen in the tree, muffled in spiderwebs. He was terrified, and he seized her by the neck and pushed. Her nails ripped the skin from his arms. He pushed harder, and blood began to spill from her mouth. Then suddenly he realized that he was choking a frog. The frog was dead. He stood up. The blood was still oozing from its mouth.

Qaqo began to run through the forest. He ran all the way up the trail, and did not stop until he reached the highway. It was getting dark and all his kif was gone. He hurried on to Tchar ej Jdid. His mother was waiting for him.

Did you see the affrita? she asked him.

There was no affrita, said Qaqo. There was nothing at all.

THE DUTIFUL SON

A youth named Mehdi who came from the place of a hundred and one saints married a girl from Temsaman as beautiful as he was handsome. They lived on a farm where nothing grew but almond trees and kif. Their first child was a girl whom they named Zohra. She stayed with them for a little more than a year, and then she fell ill with a sickness in her throat. There were no doctors in that part of the country, so they did not know what was the matter with her. They gave her many sorts of herbs that grow in the mountains, but it did not help her. A terrible odor began to come out of her mouth, and she died.

Not much later a son was born to them, and they named him Mohammed. Mehdi said to his wife: I'm eighteen now, and you're seventeen. I think we should move to the city.

They went to Tangier, where Mehdi had relatives. They told him: There's a new hotel here that's taking on help. Why don't you try? He went to the Hotel Minzah and they gave him work in the kitchen as an assistant. He had brought a good sum of money with him from the sale of the farm, and he earned high wages at the hotel.

After a few months an older woman named Aicha Riffiya began to follow him around in the street, and to wait for him outside the hotel. She lived in a brothel in Bnider, but she was in love with Mehdi. And so she captured him, a young man with a son. She even showed him how to drink wine.

One night Mehdi and his friends gave a party at a mahal in Bnider. They had several women there with them. For the first time Mehdi did not sit beside Aicha Riffiya. He was paying attention to a girl named Haddouj Djibliya. He smoked kif and drank with his friends, and Aicha Riffiya sat and watched him. As she watched, hatred for Mehdi filled her heart. If she had been able to kill him then and there, she would not have waited. However, there was nothing she could do at that moment but watch.

Mehdi spent the night with Haddouj Djibliya. In the morning he went to work, and at the end of the day he went home. His wife greeted him by saying: Where were you all night? I was waiting for you. It didn't come into your head that perhaps your son was sick or that I might need you, or that maybe something had happened here in the house. You've begun to go with whores, and they've taught you to drink wine. I can smell it.

Shut up! he shouted, and he jumped up and slapped her twice, very hard. I know, she said. I have no right to speak. I'm only your wife. But I love you, and you love me, and you hit me because I tell you the truth. You hit me because you like wine and whores. You're married, Mehdi! Why do you want whores and wine? If I'd known you were like this I'd never have married you! Now I understand why you wanted to come to Tangier. Because in the Rif there are no whores. You're disgusting!

Do you want me to bash your head in?

She stopped talking and merely sobbed. Mehdi threw some money on the table and went out. He walked straight down to Bnider. Aicha Riffiya was waiting for him in the street.

Labess.

Labess. Come on in.

Mehdi went in, and they sat on piles of cushions in an inner room. Aicha Riffiya was very lively. Let's have a celebration tonight, she said.

They ordered wine and cognac, and started to drink. What with the kif and the cognac, Mehdi began to feel happy. Aicha Riffiya was waiting for this time, so that she could bring out what she wanted to give him and slip it into his glass.

When she had emptied the powder into the glass, she filled it with cognac and gave it back to him. Mehdi spent the night with Aicha Riffiya and went to work in the morning. The kitchen seemed hotter than usual. He felt a great weight inside him, and his head was swimming. Then he fell to the floor in the middle of the kitchen.

They took him to the British Hospital and the doctor gave him medicine through needles. I can't see anything the matter with this young man, said the doctor. His body is in perfect condition.

At the hospital there was a Moslem who had worked there for many years, ever since his childhood. When the old man looked at Mehdi, he shook his head and said: That boy has eaten tsoukil. He should be given very old oil.

The man himself went and got the oil, and took it to Mehdi in the hospital. When Mehdi was taken home the next day in an ambulance, he went along, carrying the oil.

After a week or so Mehdi was well. The day he got up, his wife said to him: What did you find when you opened your eyes? Who was sitting beside your bed? The whores you spend your nights with, or your wife?

It's the last time, said Mehdi. I'm never going to do it again.

When Mehdi's son was fifteen, he too began to go to Bnider, and he got to know all of his father's friends there. By then he had heard the story of what Aicha Riffiya had done to his father. One day he invited some friends to his mahal on the Hafa. They brought along some whores with them. The oldest whore was Aicha Riffiya. After everyone was drunk, the boy stood up and said: My father was handsome and he owned a diamond. That was my mother. And you, Aicha Riffiya, wanted to kill him because one night he went off with another whore like you. But he didn't die.

And the boy rushed at her, and pulled off her pants, and wrenched open her legs, and burned her with the Lucky Strike he was smoking. They all laughed while she screamed. Then two of his friends got up and stopped him. That's enough, they told him. The cigarette is broken, anyway.

Aicha Riffiya was not able to walk for two weeks. When Mehdi heard of it, he said: I never paid her back, but my son did. He's a good boy.

BAHLOUL

There was a young man they called Bahloul, who lived alone with his mother. His father had left home when he was four years old. Since then his mother had cared for him, working in the house of some Nazarenes. When he was ten, she had bought a small house with a patch of land around it. Now, she said, at last I can relax. I've got my own house, and if I should die, you'd have a place to live, aoulidi.

I wish I knew where my father was, said Bahloul.

If he's still alive, he'll come back to find you, she told him. Or if he's dead, we'll see him when we all go before Allah.

When Bahloul was fifteen, his mother fell ill and took to her bed. He was overcome by anxiety. There was no one else in the house, and he stayed home from school to take care of her.

Then the Nazarenes she worked for came to see her, and they called an ambulance and had her taken to the hospital. For three months she stayed there, while Bahloul lived at home by himself. He did not go back to school, but instead sat with his friends in a café. And when he went home at night he would take another boy along with him to sleep there, so that he would not be so afraid. Then he grew used to smoking kif, which he enjoyed every time.

One morning an ambulance drew up in front of the house. Two internes jumped down and took out a stretcher from the back. They asked Bahloul if this was the house where the sick woman lived.

I'm her son, he said.

Your mother's dead, they told him. May she stay with Allah.

Bahloul began to cry. The neighbors came and comforted him.

Don't cry. It's bad. And you're a man now.

They carried her inside and laid her on the bed. Bahloul took the key to the box where she had kept her money, and opened it. He pulled out a little money and locked the box again. Then he went out of the house and down to the city. On the way he met his friend Zizi. Where are you off to?

I've got to go and buy a kfin for my mother before I take her to the cemetery.

Shall I go with you?

Let's go.

They went down to the city, and Bahloul bought the kfin, five meters long, and rose water, sandalwood and bakhour. And he bought many figs and loaves of bread. Then they walked back to the house, left everything inside, and went to the mosque.

Bahloul asked the fqih if he would bring some tolba at the hour of the evening prayer, to chant for his mother. The fqih said he would.

To Zizi he said: Tell your mother to get some couscous ready. He and Zizi went and bought all the ingredients: the meat, vegetables and spices, and took them to her, and she prepared the couscous. At twilight the fqih arrived at Bahloul's house with all the tolba.

Bahloul showed them into a room, and they began to chant the Koran. Every corner of the house smelled of sandalwood, and the smoke poured out into the street. The tolba stayed until the dawn prayer. Then they all filed out and walked to the mosque to pray together.

In the morning two women came to Bahloul's house and washed his mother. And they dressed her all in white and prepared her for the cemetery. The tolba returned to the house. They put her onto a litter and carried her out.

At that moment Bahloul felt again like crying. But instead he began to laugh. He walked behind the litter to the cemetery, and watched them bury his mother. Afterward he gave the bread and the dates to the people waiting there in the cemetery. This was his sadaqa.

Three days later Bahloul asked Zizi's mother to make couscous again. This time he needed a great quantity of it. When it was ready he carried it to the cemetery, and to the mosque, and to his own house. The tolba came again to chant and eat couscous. Then it was all over.

In the morning when he got up, Bahloul went straight to the café. Make me a glass of tea, he said to the qahouaji. Then he ran out and bought some pastries to eat with the tea. Make me another tea, he said. He pulled out a small sebsi and his mottoui, and smoked.

An elderly man named Ali came in.

Good morning, Uncle Ali, said Bahloul.

Bahloul, my son!

Ali, can you sell me some aghrebia? The kind you always make? The time I tried them I thought they were fine.

Ouakha, my son. If you want some, I'll make them.

How much will it cost?

It's a little expensive now, Ali said.

How much?

I can make a few, maybe twenty or thirty, Ali began.

No. More. How much for fifty?

That would cost you three hundred pesetas.

Bahloul pulled the money out of his pocket. Here you are. Make them a little hard, can you?

If they're hard I'll get only forty out of it. Anyway, it'll be one batch, and no more.

Ouakha, Uncle Ali. Bahloul took out another twenty-five pesetas and gave it to him. Here's a tip for you.

Ali took the money, and Bahloul got up, paid for the teas, and went out. From the café he walked to Sidi Boukhari. On the way he met Zizi, who wanted to know where he was going.

I thought I'd go down to the city and look around for a half a kilo of kif.

Let's go. I'll go with you, said Zizi.

In the Medina they found the kif, and Bahloul bought half a kilo and the tobacco that came with it. When they walked into the Zoco de Fuera they saw the Nazarenes in whose house Bahloul's mother had worked. The Nazarenes called out to Bahloul. He went over and spoke to them.

We've been twice to your house to look for you, they told him. But both times you were out. Can you come to our house on the Mountain tomorrow? We want very much to see you. We're going away.

All right, said Bahloul. I'll see you tomorrow.

The two boys went back to Bahloul's house. Since his mother had fallen ill he had arranged one of the rooms for himself the way he wanted it, with five stuffed owls on the wall and four sheepskins on the floor. He put some water on to boil. Then he and Zizi sat down to pull the leaves and dry parts from the kif stalks, leaving only the bunches of flowers. Bahloul prepared the tea and poured it, and the two began to smoke.

As they were smoking, Bahloul suddenly said: Zizi, I want to buy a store. My poor mother left a little money behind. If I go on spending it, it'll be finished and I'll have nothing. You know me. I have no trade. I can't do anything.

Why not have a shop? said Zizi. You know how to buy and sell.

Yes, that's what I'll do.

When they had finished preparing and cutting the kif, each one filled his mottoui with the fresh mixture.

Where do you want to go now? Bahloul asked Zizi.

Why don't we sit a while in the café?

The café. Always the café, complained Bahloul. Why can't we go and see a movie?

Ouakha, if you like.

They walked down to the Zoco de Fuera, and went into the Joteya to a café that belonged to El Amartsi. They sat down and called to him. Bring us two black coffees, Moroccan style. They smoked, and talked with the other clients about *isti'amar*, which was what everyone discussed in those days when the French ruled Morocco.

When evening came, they walked down the Calle de Italia to where the cinemas are. Finally they chose the Capitol, because there was a film showing the war between America and Germany. They enjoyed seeing the part about Hitler when he was a boy.

Zizi, that's what we've got to do to France some day. If we want to get her out of here we've got to make a war like that, Bahloul whispered.

When the film was over they decided to go to a bacal. They bought bread and a can of tunafish, and made sandwiches. On the way to Bahloul's house they passed a café in the neighborhood that was still open, and went in. They ordered tea to drink with the sandwiches. Then they went to the house. One of them slept on one mtarrba, and the other on another, and the night passed.

In the morning Zizi, before washing or eating, filled his kif-pipe and began to smoke.

Zizi, that's bad for you. You've got to eat something first. Then smoke, and it won't hurt you. Not like that.

I'm used to it, Zizi told him. Remember, I'm seventeen. When he had smoked four pipes he got up and washed his face. Then they went out together to a café, and Bahloul bought ten pastries. Zizi could eat only two of them because he had been smoking, and Bahloul ate the rest, and ordered an extra glass of tea.

Your stomach is shut, Bahloul told Zizi.

While they sat there Ali came into the café. He had a large box in his hand with the forty aghrebia in it. Here are your forty, my son, he said. You've got twenty pesetas coming to you.

Give me the aghrebia and keep the twenty pesetas.

At three in the afternoon Bahloul and Zizi climbed up the Mountain to see the Nazarenes. Bahloul rang the bell. A maid answered. Is the señora here?

Wait.

The Nazarene woman appeared in the doorway. Come in, she said, and they followed her into the house. What would you like? Whiskey, beer, wine?

Thank you. We don't drink, Bahloul said.

We're leaving Morocco, you see, and we're not coming back. It's too bad, but that's how it is. We have work to do in America, so we've got to go. But there's no place like Morocco, and we're all very sad.

Then she brought out a large sheet of paper and laid it in front of Bahloul. Here, she said. Sign your name at the bottom here. And I'll sign mine. You see? Now, all these things here are for you. You can take them all away. We've sent everything else to America, and at seven thirty tomorrow we're taking the plane. But you must keep that paper. It's very important for you.

Bahloul was delighted. He folded the paper and put it into his pocket.

We loved your mother, and we want to give you something worthwhile. She handed Bahloul a check.

Your mother was with us for a long time. She was a brave woman. Very clean, and a fine worker. Like one of the family to us. When I saw her son left all alone in the world, I felt very bad, and I wanted to help. You must excuse me for saying all this in front of your friend, but there's no time.

On the contrary. You're doing me a great favor, said Bahloul. He and Zizi went to get a large truck which they brought back with them to the Mountain. They began to carry out the furniture and other things. They drove the truck to Bahloul's house, emptied it, and returned to get more.

At his house he filled the three rooms he did not use. Finally they were completely full of furniture and rugs. They had even brought pails and brooms, and all the flower pots from the garden. They left the house on the Mountain completely empty. Bahloul wished the Nazarenes a good journey, said good-bye, and went home to bed.

Early the next morning he and Zizi went together to the bank to cash the check, and got the money. I'm really happy now, Bahloul told Zizi. I've got a little cash, and I'm going to rent the shop next door. Let's go and see the owner.

They went to the man's house and knocked on the door.

Salaam aleikoum.

Aleikoum salaam. What is it?

I'd like to rent the empty shop down the street.

What for?

I want to sell things in it.

I see. It's a hundred pesetas a month.

Bahloul gave the man a thousand pesetas. Now it's mine for a long time. Please give me a receipt, then. Say I paid ten months in advance.

The man wrote out the paper and gave him the key to the shop.

Bahloul and Zizi walked down to the city. They came back with a truck full of sugar, flour, oil, tea and cans of food. They bought a pair of scales for weighing the food, and everything else that was necessary for opening a store. The next morning they were both there, and the door was open so that customers could come in.

The first week they sold a great deal of merchandise. The two sat there all day in the shop drinking tea and smoking kif and eating pieces of aghrebia, which was stronger than the kif. The neighbors would send their children for a kilo of sugar or two kilos of potatoes or a bottle of oil or a liter of kerosene. At the end of the month my father will come and pay you, the children said.

They noted down every sale, and more people came, and they noted down what they took and how much they owed. Out of a hundred customers maybe twenty-five would pay, and the rest promised to pay at the end of the month. And at the end of the month the men would come and say they could pay only half. Each time

Bahloul did the accounts, he found that he had lost more money, and this went on month after month.

At the end of the year he realized that he had lost about twenty thousand pesetas. The neighbors had them.

Bahloul did not wait. He sold everything in the store and returned the key to the owner. He was disgusted with his life, and sat around the house in a very bad humor. Zizi said to him: That was a good business we had, wasn't it? We couldn't even get our money out of it.

I'm not going to fight with them, said Bahloul. If they want to give me my money they will. If they don't, Allah will know what to do with them.

And we'll stay together up to the last franc, said Zizi.

They were sitting in a café. Suddenly Bahloul said to the owner: Do you want to sell your café?

Now that you mention it, I do. Do you want it? I'll sell it to you.

How much?

Cheap. A hundred thousand pesetas with the chairs and everything.

That's not cheap, said Bahloul.

And how much can you give?

Seventy thousand.

The man thought for a while, and then he said: I'll sell it. They went that day to the adoul and arranged the papers, and the man sold Bahloul the café. The following morning they took possession of it. Bahloul made the tea and coffee, and Zizi served it. Business was very lively. All the young men of the neighborhood began to come regularly. Let us say that fifty young men came every day, and twenty of them never paid.

Bahloul always brought an aghrebia with him from the house, which he shared with Zizi. Usually they made one cake last for two days. This way they were always happy, no matter what the hour of the day. But each time Bahloul went over the accounts, he flew into a rage. Finally he could not stand it any longer.

Zizi, he said. You go on working. I can't work here any more.

Ouakha, Zizi said. You take care of buying everything, and I'll do the work in the café. See if you can earn any money. I don't believe it.

Bahloul did not work any more. He sat in the corner smoking kif, drinking tea, and eating his aghrebia. His friends would gather round him and listen to his stories. Sitting there with them one day, he said: Now I'm going to tell you a tale, and it's a true one.

Who'd it happen to? You?

If it didn't happen to me, it happened to somebody just like me, Bahloul said.

What's the story?

This one smoked kif, lots of it, and took hashish, even more of it. And when he was alone in his house with his head bubbling with kif and hashish, he would go into an empty room to drink his tea. Afterward he would take the wet mint and tea leaves out of the teapot and scatter them over the floor. There was one window in the room, and it looked out onto an orchard that belonged to a Djibli. The Djibli had built bee-hives under the trees. So this one would open the window and let the bees fly into the room. They would all come in and light on the floor where the mint leaves were because they liked the sugar. And he did this every day. But at the same time he was busy building a whole set of hives along the walls of the room. One day when he opened the door into the room he saw everything black with bees. He went over and shut the window. Then he shut the door and bored a hole in it, and fitted the hole with a cork. The bees stayed in the room, and he threw sugar and other food for them through the hole. And the light came in the window for the bees.

The bees filled all the hives along the walls with honey. Then they filled the corners of the room. The room was covered with honey, and he began to wonder how he was going to get it out without being stung.

And Bahloul asked his friends: How could he do it? How do you think?

He put on special clothes to do it.

No.

He opened the window and the bees flew out.

No, no.

He smoked them out.

No, said Bahloul.

How did he do it, then?

First he ate a lot of majoun and smoked a lot of kif. Then he took off all his clothes, and got out a jar of honey he had bought in the souq. And he rubbed honey everywhere over his body, over his hair and his skin, everywhere. And he took two pails and went inside the room and shut the door after him. The bees came and swarmed over him, but not one of them stung him. Then he pulled out the combs of honey from the hives and took them outside. A lot of the bees were stuck to him. They couldn't move. When he stood outside in the wind for a while they began to drop off.

He put the combs into a barrel, washed himself off, got dressed, and went to wring the wax out of the honey. In the end he had about a hundred kilos of honey. Then he went out to the nearest shop and said to the baqal: Do you want to buy some pure honey? The baqal was sitting with the Djibli who owned the orchard, and they both began to laugh. Where would a hacheichi like you get honey? they said. But he told them: If you don't believe it, try some. And he opened a jar he'd brought with him. If you can't tell whether it's pure, bring an expert, he told them.

The baqal took a taste of the honey and turned to the Djibli. You're the bee man. You try it, he told him. And the Djibli tried it and said: That's pure, all right. Then he sighed and said: I don't know what's the matter with my bees this year. They're not doing very well.

Yes, the hacheichi said. I wonder what happened to them. They're all in my house. I cleared out my bedroom for them, and I'm sleeping in the bathroom.

What? cried the Djibli. What do you mean?

That's right, he said. You know, bees don't like stingy men. You always kept all their honey for yourself and never gave any to your neighbors. They don't like that, so they came to me.

If you've got my bees I'm going to the government, the Djibli told him.

What government? You tell the government and I'll tell Allah. My window was open. The bees flew in and I shut the window. Is that the government's business? Or yours? The bees are living with me now and I'm giving them food and lodging, and your government has nothing to do with it. Do you want to buy some honey? And the hacheichi sold ten kilos to the baqal. The Djibli waited a while, and then he went to his orchard. He walked over to the window of the hacheichi's house and broke the glass with a rock. The bees were upset, and they came out and swarmed over his face and stung him all over, and he began to run through the orchard yelling. If he hadn't had a well there he'd have been stung worse. When he jumped in half the bees flew off and the other half drowned. His sons came and fished him out.

When the hacheichi got home and opened the door of the room to feed the bees, they were all gone. He looked up and saw the broken window. Then he ran out into the orchard, and the Djibli's sons came up to him, crying: Your bees almost killed our father.

He threw a rock at the window and the bees didn't like it. They didn't need any government. Allah takes care of them, and He'll take care of your father.

Bahloul stopped talking.

That's a new idea, they said. Rub yourself with honey. But which was talking just now? The aghrebia or the kif?

Both, said Bahloul. That night he said to Zizi: I'm going to eat with you here and go home to bed. I've got to get up at five tomorrow morning. I'm going to Tetuan.

Zizi bought a kilo of smelts and sent them out to the oven to be baked. They ate them together and drank a little tea. Then Bahloul gave Zizi the key to the house. I'm going to bed.

He went home, had two pipes of kif, and fell asleep before Zizi arrived. He did not hear Zizi come in, nor did Zizi hear him when he got up at four o'clock in the morning and left the house. He went to the Avenida de España where he found a taxi about to leave for Tetuan. He got in with the other three passengers.

This was the first time Bahloul had been to Tetuan, and when he arrived he began to wander through the narrow streets of the Medina. It was only about half past seven in the morning, and the air was still cold. In one of the alleys a man lay on the ground asleep. Bahloul stopped and looked down at him. He was old and dirty, and his djellaba was ragged and worn thin. Bahloul looked down at his face, and suddenly felt a great surge of pity for the man. He leaned over and woke him out of his sleep.

The man sat up and stared at him. What do you want, my son?

Sidi, I saw you lying there like that, sleeping on the stones in the cold, and I felt sorry for you.

That's how Allah wants it, said the man. Hamdoul'lah!

You're right, said Bahloul. Hamdoul'lah! Come and have breakfast with me.

The man stood up, and they walked together down the street to a café. Bahloul bought pastries and they drank tea. He pulled out his pipe, and he and the old man began to smoke together.

57

Tell me your story, said Bahloul. What happened to you? Have you always lived here like this?

No, my son. And I'm not from here. I'm from Tangier. I was married, and I even had a son. But one day my wife came to me and said she wanted to work. I was making plenty of money then working in the port. But I drank, and I went with the whores. And when she came and told me she was going to work so she could buy what she needed for herself, I told her she was not going to work. And we had a fight. Aoulidi, I left her and the boy, and we weren't divorced, either.

Bahloul said: How old was the boy, sidi, when you left him?

He was four. Still very small. I don't know whether he's still alive or dead long ago. Some friends came a few years ago and told me my wife was working at the house of some Nazarenes on the Mountain.

The man went on with his story, and mentioned the name of the Nazarenes. Then Bahloul knew that the man was his father. What quarter did you live in? he asked him.

We lived in Ain Hayani.

Ain Hayani. What house?

Moqaddem Larbi.

Bahloul said: I know that house.

You do? cried the old man. And do you know the woman?

The poor woman died some time ago. I didn't know she had a son.

Bahloul felt very sorry for the man in front of him. But when he told himself that this was his father, he decided to say nothing. He took out some money and handed it to the man. Come with me to Tangier and I'll give you work, he told him. But first take this and buy some clothes and go· to the hammam and wash, and have the barber shave you. Then come back here.

Yes, my son. I'll go with you.

And Bahloul took the old man with him to Tangier. The first place they went was Ain Hayani. Bahloul stopped in front of the house where he lived. Was it there? he asked him.

Yes. It was there.

They went to Bahloul's café. This is mine, he told him. Would you like to work here? I'll pay you. You'll eat what I eat. There's a small room in the back where you can sleep.

Thank you, my son. You're very kind.

58

Bahloul called Zizi over and told him: This old man is going to stay in the café and take care of it. You and I can have a good rest and travel a little. I'm fed up with the noise and people. We'll get away from them. The new man can take of them for us all right. I trust him.

THE SPRING

A husband and wife lived in the country. When the woman needed water she went down the hill to a spring to get it. The spring water was sweet and clean. They could wash in it and drink it.

One day when the woman went to the spring she found a frog sitting on a stone there. She filled her pail and went back up to the house.

Her husband came in, and she said to him: Today when I went down to the spring I saw a frog there. In the five years we've been living here I've never seen a frog. And today I did.

If there's a frog there, that is Allah's will, her husband told her. No one knows His way. The poor thing probably came from somewhere else, and found the spring and liked it. Or perhaps it was thirsty. Don't touch it. It won't do any harm. If you see it there, just fill your pail and come back to the house.

The next day when the woman came up from the spring she said to her husband: I saw the frog there again.

Just leave it alone, he said. Don't pay it any attention.

Ya, rajel, she said. If we leave that frog there, it will go into the water and maybe lay eggs, and then there will be a lot of small frogs. And when they grow larger, the water will be dirty and we won't be able to drink it. It will always be dirty,

I'll buy a chemical and spread it around the edge of the spring. That ought to keep it away. I'll sprinkle it on the rocks outside, so it won't poison the water. The frog won't be able to get near the spring. If it tries to, it will die,

60

That's a good idea, she said.

The next day the woman went down to the spring. The frog was sitting in the place where she always stooped down to fill her pail. She raised the pail and brought it down on the frog. And as the pail struck the frog the frog cried out, and it was like the cry of a person. She looked, but the frog was gone. She filled her pail quickly and went to the house.

I found the frog down there, she told her husband. It was right where I always fill my pail, and so I hit it. I hit it with the pail. And when I lifted up the pail again, it was gone!

Allah! cried her husband. That was not a frog you hit! It was something from the dark. I told you to leave it alone, and you wouldn't listen to me. And now you're going to have trouble. I even went and got the chemical. We could have put it there, and everything would have been all right. That way it wouldn't have done us any harm afterwards.

Well, now I've hit it, she said. And it's gone away without doing anything.

All we can do is pray to Allah that nothing happens, he told her.

The woman stayed away from the spring for ten days. Then one morning she said to her husband: Ya, rajel! I'm going down now to the spring and get a little water. It's a long time since I've been down there.

All right, he said. Go down. Go on.

She took the pail in her hand and walked down to the spring. First she washed the stones in front of it. She dipped the pail into the water and filled it, but when she tried to lift it out again, she found that she could not move her arm.

She began to call to her husband. He heard, and came running down to the spring.

What is it?

I can't move my arm!

Her arm was dead. Then it began to twitch and shake. Look, rajel! she cried. See how it's moving!

That day the man put his wife on a donkey. He led it down to the road until he came to the highway. Then he stopped a Frenchman who was driving past. He asked him to carry him and his wife to the hospital.

He told the doctor the story. The doctor looked at her arm and took blood from it. He stuck needles into her and gave her many kinds of pills. None of it did her any good.

People told him: You should take her to Moulay Yacoub.

He took her to Moulay Yacoub. Nothing.

Then people said: You should take her up to Sidi Hassein.

He took her up to Sidi Hassein. Nothing.

Then they told him he must kill a black bull. He bought a black bull and led it down to the spring. There he cut its throat so that the blood would fall into the water, and then he cooked the meat without salt, and when night came he put a big dish of the unsalted meat in front of the spring.

He gave the rest of the meat to the poor and to holy men and teachers. And nothing.

One day a friend came to visit him. There's a fqih in Beni Makada you ought to go to, he told him. He'll be able to help you.

The man took his wife to the fqih in Beni Makada. The fqih read his books and looked at the woman. Finally he said: You must call in some Gnaoua once a year. If this is not done, you will get worse. Now only your arm is moving by itself like that, but in a little while it will be your whole body. The only thing to do is to have the Gnaoua in once a year and kill a black bull for them and eat its flesh without salt. No salt.

The man decided to do this. He bought a bull and cut its throat, and cooked it without salt. And he called in the Gnaoua.

The Gnaoua began to dance, and soon the woman entered their world, and was dancing like them. And the moment she began to dance, her arm stopped shaking.

The Gnaoua were singing and beating their drums, and she was dancing. And she ate the unsalted flesh. They brought a long platter heaped with slices of raw meat that was wet with blood. And while she ate she went on dancing, and she covered her face with the blood. She kept eating until she had cleaned the platter of all the meat and blood.

The chief of the Gnaoua got up and passed his hands over her face, but she danced and danced, and went on dancing and dancing, until she fell onto the ground. And she was screaming, and her legs were kicking and twitching. At last she lay still, like a dead woman.

When the Gnaoua had finished their work, they went home. The man put the woman to bed, and she stayed there, asleep. When she awoke, she got up, and her arm was a little better.

The next year they called in the Gnaoua again, and again her arm was better.

The third year when they had the Gnaoua, they invited many people. While the Gnaoua were dancing and singing, a man appeared among them, and none of the guests could say who he was. The Gnaoua stopped playing and were quiet.

The man stood in front of the woman as she danced, and spoke to her.

You struck my son. You broke his arm.

The woman stopped dancing.

I've never hit anyone, she said. And I've never broken anybody's arm. I live alone with my husband in the country here. My neighbors live far away.

You hit my son with your pail and broke his arm.

Then she remembered the frog. I hit a frog, she said.

That was my son. He went to get a drink of water and you hit him.

I found that frog there several times, she said. I never wanted to hit it. But that day I found it sitting on the stone where I used to fill my pail. I made it go away.

The man said: Now his arm is broken, and if it stays like that, I promise you more trouble.

I shall fight you to the end, she told him. Until one or the other of us is finished, your son or I.

The man turned and disappeared into the crowd. The Gnaoua began to play again, and the woman started to dance, and she danced and danced. After a while, she gave a great leap into the air and landed face down on the ground. The chief got up, passed his hands over her face a few times, and then covered her with a white sheet. The others dragged her into a room.

In the morning when she awoke, she found her arm better. She went on visiting many fqihs, and they wrote out papers for her to wear around her neck. And she went to see many tolba, and they wrote words for her. She made trips to the tombs of the saints. She would take a little earth from near the tomb, carry it home, and put it into a glass. Then she would mix water with it and drink it. And she always dropped money into the hands of the poor who were lying in the street.

Three years went by, and she gave birth to a daughter. And each year they had the Gnaoua in. She and her husband were finally happy. The woman's health was much better, and her arm did not

63

shake as it had done before.

One day she took the baby and strapped it to her back, so she could go out. She walked down to the spring, filled the pail, and carried it up to the house. Then she began to scrub the floor.

Soon her husband came in. When she saw him, she said to him: Take the baby off my back.

She's all right there. Leave her there.

Take the baby off! she cried.

He lifted the baby off its mother's back and laid it on the bed. The woman turned and went out of the house. She walked through the orchard and sat down under a tree. She began to talk to herself.

Trin, trin. Trin, trin, she was saying, all alone under the tree.

Her husband went out behind her through the orchard. When he got to the tree he found her sitting there by herself, talking. He stood still and watched her, and he wondered what had happened to her. In all the years he had lived with her he had never seen her sit alone talking to herself.

When she turned her head to look at him, he saw that her eyes had grown red and were pushing out of her face. She jumped up. Then she put her hands around his neck, trying to choke him. He led her into the house.

What's the matter? What's happened to you? he was saying. He lighted some bakhour for her, and went out to look for a fqih, or anyone who might be able to help her.

The baby was still lying on the bed. The woman got up and went over to sit beside the baby. She leaned over it, and then she bit a big piece out of its thigh.

Eat, eat! Go on eating! Eat, eat, with bones and all! Crunch them!

When her husband returned with a fqih to help her, she had already eaten half the baby. The fqih held her while her husband ran to call the police.

They came and carried her out. A doctor examined her. I can't find anything wrong with this woman, he told them. They say she's crazy, but I don't see anything the matter with her. Her blood is healthy. She has no bad disease, no syphilis, nothing. The woman is clean and strong. Her brain is in good condition.

We'll put her in jail, the police said.

They locked her into a cell. When they came to bring her food they found her lying on the floor. They tried to wake her up, but she did not move. Then they called in her husband. You had better take your wife out of here, they said. It looks as though she would be dying soon.

They carried her to an ambulance, drove her back to the country, and left her at home. For about two months she stayed in bed. Her arm had grown twisted and stiff, and one leg was shrivelled. When she got up, she walked in all directions, and she did not know what she was doing.

Each year her husband went on calling in the Gnaoua, and then they would give her the raw meat wet with blood. Whenever she could catch a cat in the orchard, she would eat it, all of it. Or a small dog. If she had been able to she would have eaten people.

Her husband decided to take her again to see the doctor. They kept her in the hospital for about two weeks. It did no good. When she came out, she was always falling down, and then she would lie kicking and screaming.

The woman is not crazy, the doctor would say. She's not crazy.

Then her husband set out on the pilgrimage to Mecca. That year he did not call the Gnaoua in to dance.

There was a shed in the orchard, behind the house. One morning not long after her husband had gone away, she went inside the shed and shut the door. She had a candle with her. She lighted it and stuck it on top of a trunk that was there. Then she lay down on an old mattress in the corner and fell asleep.

The shed was full of straw for the goats and cows to eat in the winter. When the candle burned down, the wick fell onto the straw and caught fire to it.

The woman went on sleeping until the whole shed was burning around her. She tried to get up from the mattress, but with her stiff arm and her crooked leg, she could not move fast enough.

The neighbors saw the smoke and came running down the road. They broke the door of the shed and found her with her face and body burned black, and they dragged her outside. The police came and said she was dead.

Her family arrived, washed her and wrapped her in a winding-sheet. They carried her on a litter to the cemetery and put her into the earth.

When her husband returned from Mecca, the people of the village told him: Your wife is dead. And they told him how she died.

Yes, he said. No one can live in that house, or in that orchard. The place is dangerous. It's part of the dark world.

THE BOY WHO SET THE FIRE

In Al Hoceima lived two men who were both kif-smokers. Because of this they were very good friends, and shared a house. One of them was single and the other was married and had a small son. Ali, the married man, went to work in the morning, while Ouallou the bachelor worked at night. Ali went out each morning leaving Ouallou asleep. When Ouallou woke up he would find himself alone in the house with Ali's wife, and they would sit and talk together. They did this for many months before anything happened between them. Then Ouallou suggested to the woman that she divorce her husband and marry him.

For a long time I've been thinking the same thing, she said. I didn't dare say anything for fear you might tell Ali, and he'd kill me.

How do you think we should manage the divorce? he asked her.

We won't bother with that, she told him. We'll give him something in his food. It's easier. And then there'll be just the two of us.

Ouallou went out and searched until he found the right plants, and then he took them back to the woman. That night she prepared the herbs and put them in Ali's coffee.

As soon as he drank it, he began to have pains. They grew worse. Soon he was rolling on the floor and screaming. The woman stood and watched him die. In the morning she wailed with her family while they carried him away to the cemetery.

Forty days later she and Ouallou were married. They continued to live in the house, and the boy grew up with them. He was already seventeen when one of the neighbors remarked in front of him that the man who lived with his mother was not his father.

What do you mean, he's not my father?

But your father died when you were a baby, they told him. You didn't know that, Mouh? Your mother married this man later.

She did? Mouh could not believe it.

Of course, they said.

Mouh went home to see his mother.

Mother, where's my father?

Your father is dead, aoulidi. But Ouallou is your father now.

I want to see his grave, said Mouh.

The next day they went together to the cemetery, and she led him to his father's grave. Then she went home, leaving Mouh standing by the tombstone. He sprinkled water over the grave and laid some sprigs of myrtle there.

When Mouh returned to the house, his mother was waiting for him. Now that you know about your father, you should have his things, she told him. She gave him the mottoui and the kif pipe that had belonged to his father, and Mouh went to his room and began to smoke, one pipe after another. It was not long before he was sobbing. I've got to find out how he died, he thought. Did he die in his sleep, or was he sick? Or was it something else?

After a few days of thinking about it, he decided to visit a fqih and ask him some questions. There was only one fqih he trusted, and he lived in Temsaman.

One morning he got onto his horse and started out for Temsaman. In the afternoon he arrived and sought out the fqih.

What do you want, my son?

I've come to you, sidi, to find out how my father died.

Ouakha, my son. Sit down.

Mouh talked with the man for a few minutes. Then the fqih put bakhour into a lighted brazier. He took out a book and read aloud from it. After a while he turned to Mouh and said: My son, your father's death was not natural. His hour had not come. He was poisoned.

Mouh got up and said: Many thanks, sidi. How much do I owe you?

The fqih said: You may give me whatever you want.

Mouh took a hundred pesetas out of his pocket and handed them to him.

Don't go and do anything you shouldn't do, the fqih told him. If someone has sinned, Allah will punish him. Allah is the one who decides.

I'm not crazy. I'm not going to do anything. And Mouh said goodbye to the fqih. He mounted his horse and started out for Al Hoceima. It was night by the time he got home. He put his horse in the stable and went into the house.

His mother was waiting for him. Where have you been, aoulidi? she cried. I've been so worried about you!

I took a ride to Temsaman.

Come and have some dinner.

No, no. I'm tired. I want to sleep.

His mother returned to bed, and Mouh went into his room and began to go carefully through his possessions. He picked out all the things he wanted. Then he went to sleep.

In the morning he was busy carrying his things to the house of a friend. He had to make several trips during the day, taking care that his parents did not see him. That night when they were asleep, he and his friend carried out the heavy chest that had been his father's, but where Ouallou now kept his money. They hid the chest in the friend's house along with Mouh's other possessions. Then Mouh went and opened the stables. He led out several cows and horses and put them in a pasture not far away.

In the stables there were piles of straw. Mouh spread the straw through the house, and piled it outside along the walls. Then he soaked the straw with kerosene and set it afire. Since the house was built of wood, it was soon ablaze. When Ouallou and his wife awoke, there was no way of getting out, and they were burned.

The neighbors came running and shouting, but it was only a short time before the house and everything in it lay in ashes. Mouh stood there with the neighbors watching. How did it happen? they asked.

I was coming up from down below, and I saw the smoke, and I came running. All I was able to save was some of the animals.

Then he added to himself: But I didn't save *them*. They got what they deserved. They're burned.

Now that Mouh had some money, his friend let him live on at his house. He stayed there for two years while he waited for the right moment to sell his horses and cows. When he had sold them, he took the money to Tangier and bought a small house. There he filled a front room with charcoal, onions, garlic and mint, and spent his time sitting in the middle of the shop, black with charcoal dust, smoking his father's kif pipe and filling it from his father's mottoui.

MIMOUN THE FISHERMAN

A man who lived in Beni Makada used to go every day with his son to fish. All day they would stand on the rocks holding their poles, and when they were finished, the man would send the boy Mimoun home with the fishing gear, while he himself carried the fish to the market. One stormy day he slipped on a rock and fell into the sea. The waves were crashing against the cliffs, and the man could not climb out. Each time he tried, a big wave would hurl him against the rocks, and soon, while Mimoun watched, he was dead.

Another fisherman who lived nearby hired the boy to work for him on his boat. He paid him well, so that he had no reason to look for other work. After two years, however, he decided to leave. Then he began to fish from the rocks as his father had done. He would carry the pole and everything else with him, and fish all day by himself. Sometimes he brought back two baskets full of fish. He made enough by selling these to keep him and his mother and sister alive.

Early one cold morning when the east wind was roaring Mimoun stood beside the ocean casting his line. He wore his bathing-suit, and the waves broke around his chest. The fish were coming in, one after the other, and all of them big. Then he heard an automobile going along the road above. He looked up. It was a large black Mercedes, and it came to a stop. He went on fishing, the basket hanging on his arm, and he kept landing the fish. The people in the car were watching. Soon the basket was filled, and Mimoun came out of the water, wet and shivering. He set the basket of fish onto the sand, pulled out a towel and dried himself. Then he dressed, but his teeth were still chattering. He sat down, sighed. and lit a pipe of kif, As he was finishing it, he heard a man's voice calling to him.

Mimoun called back. What is it?

Have you got any fish to sell?

Yes!

Bring them up!

Why don't you come down? said Mimoun.

The man came down to the beach and began to look at the fish. He picked out the five biggest and said to Mimoun: How much are these?

Five hundred pesetas.

A hundred each?

Is that too much for you?

Yes, it is.

All right. Give me four hundred and fifty.

You're a thief! the man cried.

I'm selling to you, and you're buying, said Mimoun. He filled his sebsi and lighted it. I'm not stealing. You've got no reason to tell me I'm a thief.

When you ask such a price for fish you're stealing, the man said.

If I were going to steal, I wouldn't steal four hundred and fifty pesatas. I'd make it worthwhile. You wouldn't find me here at this time of the morning on a day like this in the water up to my neck. It's cold, and the wind is blowing, and the waves keep hitting me.

Mimoun held up his feet so the other could see the soles. Look at the cuts everywhere. They don't mean anything to you? And my clothes? I quit the work I had so that nobody would be able to tell me what to do. If I had some other work, even stealing, do you think I'd be here every day?

I'm not interested in what you do, said the man.

Oh, I know that. I was just talking. If you want to pay four hundred and fifty pesetas take the fish. If you don't, good-bye.

You'd better watch your tongue, boy. I don't think you know who I am.

Why don't you just go? said Mimoun. I haven't any fish to sell.

A second man got out of the Mercedes and came down to the beach. What's going on?

He's a robber. And he's full of bright ideas.

72

Mimoun said: I'm not going to sell you any fish. You've got five million francs parked up there on the road. And you don't want to pay the same as anybody else for fish.

The second man said: Of course we have a good car. Why shouldn't we?

Yes, why shouldn't you? Use it in good health, said Mimoun. He filled his pipe with kif and smoked it. You don't mind spending a fortune in a bar drinking whiskey, but you don't want to see any of your money go to a poor fisherman.

The two men turned and went away. Mimoun stayed where he was, sitting on the beach. He was alone, so he pulled out his thermos bottle and drank a cup of tea. Then he smoked some more kif, and ran up and down the beach for a while.

When he was warm enough, he undressed and went into the water again. He had been fishing for an hour or so when he heard the sound of the Mercedes coming back. It stopped, and he knew they were watching him as he fished.

After a few minutes the car started up and continued on its way. his second basket was full, Mimoun came out of the water. He gathered up everything and climbed over the rocks to the road. There he sat down on a stone to put on his shoes.

Suddenly the Mercedes came back from the way it had gone, and stopped not far from where Mimoun sat. A woman got out of it and walked down the road toward him.

Brother, she said. I'd like to have some of that fish.

Sister, he said, your husband or your boy-friend wanted some too, but he couldn't afford to buy any.

Don't pay any attention to him, she told Mimoun, and she laughed.

Well, pick the fish you want.

She chose six big ones and held them up. How much?

Five hundred pesetas, said Mimoun.

She took out the money and gave it to him. At that moment the second man came up. He pointed to the car. Don't you know who that man is? he said.

No. Who is he?

That's the Khalifa of Khattiya. A very important and powerful man, and you were making fun of him.

He can be whoever he is, and I'm who I am, said Mimoun. I have a right to sell my fish at any price I can get for it. Is that true or not?

That's all right, the man told him. They got into the Mercedes with their fish. As they drove past him he thought: He couldn't face me again. He had to get a woman to buy his fish for him.

RAMADAN

Ramadan's shack was in the middle of a canebrake. He lived there alone, with seven sheepskins on the floor, and on the walls he had hung things that no one else would hang, like a guerba of goatskin for water and a broken jug. He had a jacket and two djellabas made completely out of patches. He said that each garment had a hundred and one patches, and that each patch was of a different color. This may have been true.

Ramadan had a narghile made of a bottle, a stick of wood and a rubber tube. He smoked only kif in it, and he smoked all day instead of working. In order to eat he had to go to a café and try to borrow money from his friends. Give me a hundred pesetas, he would say, and I'll have them back to you tomorrow. If he got the money he would spend most of it on kif, which he smoked whole, without cleaning it or removing the seeds. Only after he had bought his kif would he get himself a little tea, a little sugar, and some bread.

One afternoon he made a small tajine. Then he went down to the Zoco Chico and walked around. Presently he met a young man whom he knew, and he invited him to go home with him. The young man agreed, and they went together to the shack in the canebrake.

What do you do all day, Ramadan? the young man asked him.

Nothing. I smoke my narghile and I sleep. And in the morning I find some money.

But who gives you the money?

I can't tell you that. If I did, I wouldn't find it any more. No, no. I can't tell you.

Ramadan made a pot of tea, lit his narghile, and they began to smoke while they sipped.

You make good tea, said the young man.

Not many people have the chance of drinking it, said Ramadan. I don't let most people into my house.

Then he brought out the tajine. All it had in it was potatoes and tomatoes. But he had a loaf of bread, and they both enjoyed the meal, because they had smoked raw kif without tobacco and they were hungry. If the meal had consisted of a boiled donkey's head, they would still have found it tasty.

When they had eaten everything, they sat back and began to smoke again. Finally they went to bed on the sheepskins. But the young man could not sleep, and he kept shifting his position. Finally Ramadan cried: What's the matter with you?

You've got something here that bites, the young man told him. Ramadan turned on the light, and they found a nest of bedbugs in the blanket.

I think I'll go, the young man said.

Have you got any money? asked Ramadan.

No.

Here's twenty-five pesetas.

The young man took the money and left, and Ramadan shut the door and went to sleep. In the morning when he got up he went to the house of a friend.

Can you lend me fifty pesetas?

The friend gave him the money. Then Ramadan went to see another man who had given him fifty pesetas another day.

Here's twenty-five pesetas, said Ramadan. Tomorrow I'll bring you the other twenty-five.

In the afternoon he went to a café. He walked to the musicians' platform and sat down. And he pulled out his narghile, set it on the floor and filled it with kif, and began to smoke it. He puffed on it once and exhaled the smoke. Ahahah! he cried. By my mother-in-law! The narghile just said to me: Take me and fill me, for the love of Sidi Hiddi!

Everyone in the café laughed, but he went on smoking. He was wearing patchwork trousers and one of his djellabas of a hundred and one colors and his cap of fifty colors. And he had with him a pouch made of seven kinds of leather. Around his neck he wore a chain with a little brass bell at the end of it. When he had kif in him he would weave his head around and make the bell ring.

A man arrived. *Salaamou aleikoum,* ya Ramadan!

At this time of day there's neither salaam nor any need for words, Ramadan told the man.

Why, Ramadan?

The kif does it.

Does what, Ramadan?

It goes into my head and comes out my ears. And my eyes turn red. I'm not inside myself. I'm outside looking in, and my heart has been scraped. No, no, no, no, no, no, no! Leave me my own dreams and my own luck.

The friend went out again, and Ramadan stayed where he was on the platform, smoking his narghile and talking to himself. At times foam would bubble out of his mouth. Soon another man came into the café, greeted the men, and then climbed up onto the soudda where Ramadan sat. And he said to Ramadan: *Salaam aleikoum.*

Now it's the time for salaaming and talking, said Ramadan. *Aleikoum salaam.* Sit down.

The man sat down. Then Ramadan lighted his narghile and handed it to his friend, saying: Smoke my pipe and call my loved one.

The man took a great puff. I've smoked your narghile and called your loved one, he told him.

Allah, Allah, Allah! cried Ramadan. No one can forget me! My name is Ramadan, and Ramadan is a long way off. But the one I love is very near.

As they went out, each one of his friends passed by him and gave him a few coins. And someone would always pay for the glasses of tea that he had drunk. He could drink as many as twenty glasses while he sat there.

When evening came he left the café and went home to his shack in the canebrake. There he spread a sheepskin on the ground and sat down in the moonlight. And he brought his teapot out and set it in front of him, and began to smoke. And he said: I'm all alone! I'm all alone! Who'll go with me? I know who'll go with me. My darling narghile, my love. But I'm afraid! I'm afraid!

He was looking up at the moon far above his head. My enemy is burned! he cried. I burned him.

And he went on lighting the narghile and smoking it, so that he spent the whole night out there among the canes, lying on the sheepskin.

In the morning he went into his shack, took out of his pouch all the money his friends had given him and tossed it onto the floor. He sat counting it for a long time. Then he washed his face, slung the strap of the pouch over his shoulder, and set out on foot for the city. There he went to an eating-stall owned by a man named El Berraq.

Give me a bowl of baisar with extra olive oil and red pepper and cumin, he told El Berraq. And a loaf of whole wheat bread to go with it.

And he ate all the bread and the baisar, and afterward he drank a litre of water. Then he took out his narghile and said to it! Good morning, darling. When evening comes, I'll say good-night to you. He stuffed the kif in, and everyone in the eating-stall was watching him, and laughing. He sucked on the tube. Allah! Allah! You hurt me! he cried. Why did you do that?

He smoked some more. There! That puff was very sweet. Wait a minute. Let me take another puff.

He sucked on the tube, shut his eyes, and murmured: Allah! That time you didn't hurt me, darling. I smoke, and you watch. I blow the smoke out, and you smell it.

Ramadan sat smoking while the others laughed. After a while he got up and tried to pay, but El Berraq told him: That's all right. Everything's taken care of.

Thank you. Allah be with you. And Ramadan went on his way down the street, until he came to Dar Debbagh. There he went into the café where the fishermen sit. At the sight of him they all began to call out: Ramadan!

Good morning to you and to me, too! he cried. And to my narghile, and to the heart of my loved one!

Yes, Ramadan. Sit down. Have a glass of tea with us.

Ramadan climbed onto the platform and joined his friends. Fill me a whole mug of it.

The qahaouaji made five glasses of tea and filled a mug. Ramadan began to puff on his narghile and sip his tea. I'm going on a trip, he told them. And it's going to be a long trip. I couldn't make it a short one.

What do you mean, Ramadan?

And a dangerous trip, too. It's far and it's near, and it's dangerous.

How, Ramadan?

Be quiet. She's listening, Ramadan whispered. She's moving. Don't talk. Don't ask questions.

What, Ramadan?

She's bad. She's very bad. She has no shame.

But who is she, Ramadan?

Death, he said.

What?

Death. She's waiting. She's here with us, moving in the room. Don't make me talk. I want to be quiet, so she won't come to me.

Then Ramadan sat quietly, merely smoking his narghile and passing it to the others. In this way they all finished by being full of kif, and each fisherman before he went out of the café gave money to Ramadan.

After a while he began again to say: I'm going on a trip. He spread out a large handkerchief with patches in it, and they threw their coins onto it. I'm going away, he said. Did you know that?

The more often he said the words, the more they gave. Some of them paid for several of his teas. At midday the fishermen cooked a tajine and invited Ramadan to eat with them. They gave him a little fresh kif, and he cut it and put it into a bladder.

Now I've got to go, he told them.

No. Stay with us a while longer. It's still early in the afternoon.

By then Ramadan had collected a good quantity of money in the handkerchief. He sat in front of them counting it. When he had finished, he said: It's enough, thanks to Allah.

He put the money into his pouch, picked up his handkerchief and his narghile, and went to the qahaouaji. I'm going on a trip, he said. I want something from you. The qahaouaji took out fifty pesetas and handed them to Ramadan.

I'll give them back to you along with many favors, he told the qahaouaji. May Allah help you! And Ramadan went out of the café.

First he went back to his shack in the canebrake and put on another djellaba over the one he was wearing. He packed his clothing, a sheepskin, some blankets, his teapot and a glass. Then he locked the shack and started walking along the road.

Night came, and he arrived at Fnidaq. He went into the woods and lay down under the trees. The jackals were howling as he fell asleep. Very early in the morning he got up and started again to walk. And he came to Tetuan, and went into a café owned by a man from Tangier.

Salaamou aleikoum!

The qahaouaji cried: Ah, Si Ramadan! Welcome! Come in. And Ramadan went in, climbed up onto the platform and sat down. He took out his teapot and handed it to the qahouaji. Fill it fast! he cried. And the man filled it for him and gave it to him, along with a plate of pastries. Ramadan ate them all and drank the pot of tea. Fill it again! he told him.

He took out his narghile and spoke to it: Good morning, narghile. And when night comes I'll stay to you: Sleep well. Ah, narghilti, you're my darling!

And he filled it with kif, lighted it, and set to work smoking. Allah! Allah! he cried.

He continued to smoke. The men of Tetuan who sat in the café looked at him, and one young man said to another: The poor man's crazy.

Ramadan heard him and burst out laughing. I'm not crazy, he said. But it might be that you are. I wasn't talking to you. I was talking to my narghile. I smoke, and then I smoke some more, and then I can see what's going on. And all that's none of your business. Yes, you may be crazy, but you're a very good-looking boy. Why don't you come and live with me?

The young man jumped up, and Ramadan laughed harder. If your grandfather had only been a man, your father might have been one, he told him. And if your father had been a man, maybe you would have been, too. But I doubt it.

The young man went out of the café very angry, because everyone was laughing. Ramadan turned to the other men. I'm very well-known, he said. And you're all very well-known. But there are many who aren't. Speak to me, narghilti, my baby! And he sucked on the pipe and blew into it, so that it bubbled, and smoke came out at the top.

Am I right or wrong? he cried to the pipe. And the water in it bubbled. What's that? I'm right? Ah, thank you! You can tell real men by their faces, and you can tell false ones by their faces. Narghilti, did you hear what the zamel said? If he'd been a man, he wouldn't have turned to his friend and said I was crazy. I was talking to you, narghilti, not to him, and he had no reason to interrupt, did he?

And Ramadan continued to smoke, and the qahouaji went on filling his pot with tea. Then Ramadan spread out his handkerchief on the platform. In the meantime he kept the men laughing, and each one left some money on the handkerchief before he went out. Then others came in, and they too began to laugh. Every so often he told them: I'm going on a trip.

About half past four in the afternoon the café was full of men from Tangier. The people of the city know each other, Ramadan said. It's too bad they've forgotten me. And why have they forgotten? Because now they have money. Money makes people forget everything. They can even forget their religion. They can forget Allah. They can forget their children. But a poor man can't forget anything. When he stops being poor he begins to rot, and he doesn't know his friends, and his heart is empty. Then it fills up with hatred. I came here to see you, and not one of you pretended you didn't know me, did you?

Si Ramadan, we're listening to you, they said.

That's what I want, said Ramadan. Who wants to smoke my narghile? Who wants to call my loved one?

Two young men got up and went to sit by him. They began to smoke the pipe. Smoke, and hold the smoke, he told them. Puff, swallow, hold the smoke. I saw a train going by, and if you don't believe me, here's its smoke. He blew out a great puff.

Ramadan went on smoking, and the men went on giving money. Finally he set to work counting it. He poured it all into his pouch and slung the pouch over his shoulder. Then he got up.

Salaamou aleikoum, he said to the men. He went to the qahouaji, who gave him money too. And he set out on the road.

By the time night came he had gone a long way, but he continued to walk half the night. Then he found an empty space between two large rocks. Here he spread his blankets and his sheepskin on the ground and slept.

In the morning he started out again through the mountains and up the valley, until he came to a village. In a field some men were sitting around a fire where a cauldron boiled. He walked over and peered into the cauldron. It was full of oats.

The men came up to him and he greeted them. I haven't eaten yet, he told them.

Yes, yes. We'll give you something, they said.

Ah, Sidi Hiddi! sighed Ramadan. Enemy of my heart! He sat

down and began to eat oatmeal. And he went on eating until he had finished four bowls of it. He smoked a bit and got up. Good-bye, and may Allah help you.

He plodded on through the mountains. It was nine o'clock in the evening when he arrived at Sidi Hiddi. He walked inside the building of the shrine where the men were sitting, and said: *Salaamou aleikoum*, men.

Aleikoum salaam, ya Ramadan, they replied.

When was the last time I came here? he asked them.

You were here two years ago, Ramadan.

And what have you been keeping for me?

Nothing, Ramadan.

Before I sit down, let me tell you, you're going to have to give me something, because I'm going on a trip.

He sat down. The last time he had been in Sidi Hiddi there had been only ten women in the sanctuary, and now there were more than thirty. And there were more Haddaoua. Si Ramadan was a Haddaoui himself, but he did not like what had been happening at the shrine during the past few years. The Haddaoua captured the women and forced them to work for them. They also allowed criminals to hide there from the police. Many of the men who had lived there for years could not go outside the shrine without fear of being captured.

Ramadan said to the chief: This is fine, what you're doing here. You're not afraid? Soon Allah will strike you from the earth. The Haddaoua here now are nothing but thieves and cutthroats. You're all criminals and slave-dealers!

The Haddaoua gave him what they said was his share, and he put the money into his pouch. Then they brought couscous, and he ate with them. When they had finished eating they brought out drums and began to beat them, and as they danced they pounded their bellies with rocks.

Yes, yes, said Ramadan. Your bellies are full of couscous, and you pound them to empty them again. Sin is ready for you. Listen, narghilti, and hear what they're doing. Don't think all this is theirs. It's all stolen.

One of the Haddaoua cried: Quiet, Ramadan! We've heard enough out of you.

Ramadan stared at him. Ah, so you're the king of the Haddaoua? You're the chief son of a whore? Do you hear, narghilti, this one is their chief now!

They stopped the music and said to him: You've got your money and you've eaten. Now you go.

You're putting me out, I see. All right. I'll go. We'll take care of this later.

Ramadan went out and started walking once more through the mountains. But two of the Haddaoua had gone out after him, and were following him. Soon he came to a river and stopped. He saw the men far behind him on the road, and put his pouch and valise down on the ground under a tree, and hid from them. When they came to the river they separated, and began to look for him. He sprang out of the bushes at one of them and knocked him into the river. When the other came running, Ramadan seized him and knocked him down. Then he bit him in the throat until the man was dead. He washed the blood from his face in the river, picked up his things, and set off again.

In the morning some Djebala passed by the river and found the drowned Haddaoui, and pulled him out of the water. Later they came across the other with his throat torn out. They carried the two bodies back to Sidi Hiddi.

No, no. It couldn't have been Ramadan, said the Haddaoua. He could never kill anyone. Some wild animal came by, and one of them saw it and jumped into the river. The other didn't see it in time, and it caught him.

All night and all the next morning Ramadan kept walking, until he came to Beni Aros. As he went into the town he noticed people whispering to each other about him. This displeased him, and so he walked through the town and went on to Beni Guerfat. There he sat down in the doorway of a café in the souk.

Soon a Spanish captain came along with four of his soldiers. As they went by, Ramadan said: Yes, yes, the Spanish do whatever they please, and our people do nothing. I wonder why that is.

The captain heard him and said to his soldiers: What's that maniac talking about?

The maniac is your grandfather. The idiot is your father, said Ramadan.

The captain tried to kick him, but Ramadan seized his leg and pushed. He toppled over, along with two of the soldiers who were trying to help the captain.

Ramadan stood up. The five of you can't do it, he said. Maybe the batallion could.

Instead of getting up off the ground, the Spanish captain drew his pistol. He tried to fire, but his finger did not move the trigger. This frightened him. When Ramadan saw it, he spat in his direction. Then he took up his things and went on his way. On the road he met some Djebala who had been in the souk and had seen everything that had happened. They gave him a donkey to ride.

When they arrived at their village, Ramadan said to the Djebala: Here's your donkey.

No, Si Ramadan, they said. It's a gift for you. He was very pleased. And he continued to ride on the donkey, until he arrived in Tangier. After that he was never seen without it. He would take his teapot and his glass and his narghile, and pile them all onto the donkey. Then he would get on, and lie on his side along the donkey's back instead of sitting astride it. As he rode through the streets he would smoke the narghile. He liked to get the donkey into the middle of the Boulevard and stop. Then he would cry out: Sidi Hiddi! You are my first love! And those who are living there with you will be destroyed! Help me, Sidi Hiddi! And he would puff harder. Speak to me, narghilti! If you don't speak, I'll know you're not mine.

And the narghile would answer: Khlukhlukhlukhlukh! The people walking along the Boulevard would laugh, and even the traffic police would laugh. Finally he would kick the donkey and go on.

Next door to Ramadan lived a very poor family. One day he went to their house and said to them: Come with me. He got on his donkey, and the family walked along behind. They went down to the Zoco Chico and into the courtyard of Dar Niaba, Ramadan still on the donkey. He tied it to the post at the bottom of the stairs and climbed up to see the notaries.

The piece of land and the shack that belongs to Ramadan of the Narghile, do you know them?

Yes, the notary said.

I want you to put the property in the name of these people I have with me. The donkey too. I want them to have everything.

The people signed the papers. Ramadan pulled out his keys. Here are the keys. You can go and live there. If you don't see me tomorrow, come to the shrine of Bou Araqia.

Ouakha, they said. Ramadan got onto his donkey and rode off. As the donkey was walking through the Zoco de Fuera, he began to cry out: Listen, people! Ramadan is leaving. Soon.

He stopped at all the cafés, including the one at Dar Debbagh, where he went into the patio. His friends looked at him and said to each other that he was very much changed.

What's the matter, Ramadan? they asked him.

I'm leaving soon. Soon. Give me a little water.

They gave him water.

Give me some tea.

They gave him tea, and he began to smoke. At nightfall he said: I'm hungry. And they brought him food, and he ate it.

Then he said: Who likes my narghile?

A young man got up. I like it, Si Ramadan.

It's for you. Take care of it, because it has great power. And when you smoke it, you'll always have good luck.

He excused himself to the others. I must go, he said.

Yes, Si Ramadan.

He went from the café to the hammam, and bathed for a long time. Then he went to the shrine of Bou Araqia. When he was alone inside, he began to talk and cry out to the shadows. He lay down beside the tomb and slept.

In the morning when the moqqadem arrived to awaken him and give him breakfast, he found him laughing. But as he came closer to him he saw that Ramadan was dead.

They buried him inside Bou Araqia, and built him a little qoubba. The poor family came the following day and took his donkey and his pouch and his clothing. And they went to his shack and lived in it, because it was better than the one where they had been living.

LARBI AND HIS FATHER

A rich Djibli farmer had two sons, Larbi and Abdeltif. The youths were very different from one another. Larbi had a bad temper, while Abdeltif was gentle as a taleb in the mosque. His father was very fond of him and spent much time with him, whereas he paid no attention to Larbi.

Larbi, who was eighteen, had four friends with whom he passed his days, smoking kif and eating majoun. Their life was like an endless feast. They took turns paying for the food and the kif. The others always had money, but often Larbi did not. His father would not allow him near the farm where the animals were kept, because he had no confidence in him. He let him eat and sleep in the house, and that was all.

One night when it was his turn to pay for the party, Larbi had neither money nor kif. He needed to buy everything, but he had nothing with which to buy it. He went to Mohammed's house and said to his friends: It's my turn and I haven't a guirch.

It doesn't matter, Larbi, they said. We're your friends and we know you. Don't even think about it. Here's the money. Here's the kif. You're our brother.

We're more than brothers, said Larbi. I know your kif is my kif, and your money is my money, and your mahal is my mahal if I want to stay in it. But I've got to have my own money in my pocket, and my own kif. When you invite me I want to invite you. The world is wrong. For every man who has money there are a hundred who have nothing. It shouldn't be that way.

You're right, Larbi. It shouldn't be that way, but that's the way it is.

Why can't the one who has it give some to the other hundred now and then?

Yes, why can't he? they said.

I'm thinking about my father, said Larbi. Allah forgive me. I'm going to tell you what I think of him. He's got thousands of acres of land, and I don't know how many sheep and cows he's got, or how many tons of wheat and fodder stored up. And the people who work for him work without pay, only for their food and a place to sleep so the rain won't wet them. And why doesn't he give them something more? Because he thinks there's no difference between them and his animals. He keeps them alive and uses them until they die. I'm going out for a while. I'll be back.

I'll go with you, said Mohammed. The two went out. It was dark, and the wind was blowing a fine rain over them. They walked up the valley, all the way to the tchar, and as they went, Larbi told Mohammed what he was going to do. When they got to the land owned by Larbi's father they went through the gate to a corral. Mohammed stayed outside the corral while Larbi went in and drove out the sheep. There were about three hundred of them in there. They took them to Mohammed's farm. The others came out then and helped them, and the five youths drove the flock all night. Getting them across the rivers was the most difficult part of the trip.

By morning all five of them were drenched with rain and smeared with mud, but they had the sheep at the souk in the city. Larbi immediately set to work selling them. The animals were unusually big and strong, and he was selling them at a low price. Soon he had got rid of them all.

Then he said to his friends: Now let's go back to the tchar. We'll look for a big taxi and have it take us back and wait while we wash and change our clothes. Then we'll come back here.

They found a taxi and drove up to their village, where they bathed and put on clean clothes. After that they returned to the city.

As they walked through the streets of the Medina, they came to a narrow alley where a woman stood. The four friends were timid country youths, but Larbi had no shame. He went up to the woman and said: *Msalkheir, lalla.*

Msalkheir, my son.

Do you live around here, *lalla?*

Yes, my son. This is my house right here.

Then Larbi said: You don't know a woman named Habiba, do you?

Yes, I know her. She used to live here in my house with me.

Larbi knew no one named Habiba. He wanted to talk with the woman.

She lived here a while, and then she moved out, she said. Was she your girl-friend?

Larbi could not say no, and so he said yes.

Well, there's better than that around here, the woman told him.

Where do you see them? he asked her. I don't see them.

The woman turned and opened the door. Come in. All five of the youths followed her inside. There were women sitting in all the rooms. Immediately Larbi saw a beautiful one, and spoke to her.

I don't want to do anything here, he told her. Can you come with me? You and four others?

Where? said the girl.

Out to the country.

She looked at him. All right, she said. I'll go. But I don't know about the others.

However, the others were willing to go, too. Larbi gave a little money to the woman who had let them in, and they all went out into the alley.

The women began to say that they needed drinks. Larbi bought some bottles of whiskey, a carton of cigarettes, and a large amount of food. Then they went to the taxi-stand. They needed two taxis to get them out to the mountains. It was a dusty drive.

Larbi paid the extra taxi and sent it away. Then he told the other driver to come back in two days to pick up the women. They opened the gate to Mohammed's orchard. Mohammed lived alone; there was no one else there. When the women went into the cabin they were surprised. It looks like nothing from the outside, and inside it's wonderful!

We're country people, said Larbi. Our houses are clean, the air we breathe is clean, and the water we drink is clean. The city's dirty, the air and the water and the life they make you live there.

That's true, said the women.

Three of the men sat down with the women. Mohammed and Larbi brought the taifor, and made a fire of logs in the courtyard. Then they took one of Mohammed's biggest sheep and slaughtered it. Quickly they pulled off the skin. Three of the women set to work washing the inside organs. Then they put them together to cook over the fire. They cut the flesh and threw it into a big cauldron. After that everyone went inside and sat down. Khemou, Larbi's friend, opened a bottle of whiskey, and Larbi brought five glasses.

Aren't you boys going to drink?

It's a sin, and we can't, Larbi said. Up here we don't know anything about alcohol. We never see it. And we can't drink it because it's forbidden. We only bought it for you. But don't misunderstand me.

Oh, no! they said. We'll drink it.

We've got our own things, Larbi told her. He brought out a big dish of majoun. The men took out their mottouis and began to smoke kif and drink many glasses of tea, while the women poured themselves whiskey.

After the women had drunk a bottle of whiskey they were happy. Mokhtar got up and unpacked a large guinbri with eight strings. Mohammed brought a bendir from the other room. When they had tuned up, they began to play together.

Soon Larbi went to the courtyard to look at the meat. It was cooked. He heaped it all on a huge platter.

He broke the bread, and they started to eat. When they had finished off all the meat, Larbi brought the cauldron of entrails that was stewing on the fire. Each woman picked a piece of liver, and Larbi and his friends ate the rest.

After they had finished eating and drunk tea and eaten more majoun, they resumed the music, and Khemou sang a *mouwal*. When she sat down afterward, Larbi was delighted. I'd like to have a wife like you, he told her. You could sing for me every day.

That's easy, she said. Tomorrow if you like.

Larbi said no more about it. They had not brought the whores to the country to marry them.

The next day was very hot, and the sun burned like fire. Larbi opened the door and stepped outside. It's summer! he cried. What a day!

They went into the orchard and washed at the well. Then they drank at the spring. Below the orchard there was a stream that ran all year. The forest began on the other side, and behind it were the mountains, with sheer cliffs of rock. The five friends stood there drying themselves and looking out over the countryside. The women were in the house getting breakfast.

When Larbi had eaten and smoked a little kif he told the others: I'm going home for a while. I'll be back.

Don't be long.

I'll walk it in no time, he said. And he climbed up the valley to his tchar.

When he got home his mother met him at the door. Where have you been all this time? she cried. Larbi!

I was staying at a friend's house, yimma.

I'm afraid for you, she said.

I'm not a woman, yimma. Why should you worry about me?

No, my son. What you're doing is not good.

What am I doing?

You're smoking kif and eating majoun. And you're sleeping away from home.

Nothing's going to happen to me.

And now what do you want?

I only came to change my clothes. He went into his room and put on fresh clothing. And he rolled up two big sheepskins and two blankets, and started to go out.

Where are you taking those things? said his mother.

I'm taking them with me. They're to sleep on and cover up with.

His father suddenly appeared at the door. Where have you been?

At my friend's house.

Your friend's house. I see. And what were you doing there with your friends?

Larbi said: What do men do, Baba?

What do you mean, what do men do? What do they do?

When you were my age, what did you do?

Son, I was working with a plow, and taking care of the sheep, and milking the cows, and studying the Koran in the mosque, and praying.

And I'm not doing anything wrong either, said Larbi. What am I doing? I smoke kif and eat majoun. There's nothing wrong with that, is there?

You can stand there and look at me and tell me you smoke kif and eat majoun? Whoever told his father such a thing?

But Baba, all those old ideas you have in your head are finished. That's not the way it is today in the world. It's a different time now. The things that used to be true aren't true any more. That's all finished.

His father opened his mouth wide and cried: Don't come any more to this house!

I was born in it and I grew up in it, and I'll come when I want to come.

There was silence. Then his father said: Where are you going with those sheepskins and those blankets?

I'll bring them back, said Larbi.

You're not taking anything out of this house! Put them down!

I've got to take them from here, Baba, because I can't get them from anywhere else. You're rich. You've got cows and sheep. And you've got twenty men working for you, and you only give them their feed, the same as you do with your livestock. They work in the dirt and feed and milk the animals, and take everything to market. And when they finish working, you feed them so they can work again.

That's not your business. What you need is to be put to work yourself.

I don't work, Baba, and I'm not going to. And when I feel like coming home I'll come home and take what I want and go out again. Excuse me, Baba. And Larbi stepped in front of his father and went out through the door, carrying with him his bundle.

In Mohammed's orchard everyone was sitting under the trees. Am I late? he said.

No! they cried. Come on and eat!

They spent the afternoon hunting for hares across the valley. That night they sat again in the room they had made under the trees. There was a full moon. They brought the pot of stew to the taifor, broke the bread, said *Bismillah*, and began to eat.

The women stayed again that night, and did not go back to the city until the following day. As they left, Larbi said to Khemou: I'll be down to see you in two days.

Ouakha, she said.

After they had driven off, Larbi told his friends: I'm going to the tchar for a while. He set off up the valley.

At home, he kissed his mother's head and sat down, with his brother Abdeltif beside him. Soon his father came in with two other men of his family. Larbi got up and kissed his father's hand. Then he sat down.

Now where have you been, son?

With my friends.

Your friends, yes. They're the ones who are going to leave you naked and begging in the street.

If you gave me money I wouldn't go on the way I am now. I'd get married and have my own sons.

It's the kif in your head that's making you talk, said his father.

It's just the opposite! cried Larbi. Kif makes you see the truth. And besides that, it makes you feel like not getting into trouble.

Words like that don't even get into my ears, his father said. Go and say them to other ears that are full of kif like yours.

The two men sitting there agreed. Why don't you listen to your father? He's an old man. Do as he tells you, as the book says.

Larbi paid no attention to them. I'm going to ask you something, Baba. I want to go and live in the city. I'd like you to help me with a little money so I can start a business.

His father burst out laughing. That's a bright idea! I give you money so you can live in the city! He laughed some more. Then he said: Not a guirch from me. If you want to go to the city, go on.

Larbi got up and went into his room. He opened a big chest and took out some money, put on his djellaba, and walked back through the other room. Good-bye, he said, and before anyone else could say anything he went out.

He was in a bad mood as he walked back down to Mohammed's farm. When he got there he went inside and sat in a corner by himself. There he smoked kif until he fell asleep. No one wanted to disturb him, and so he stayed that way until morning.

Come and have breakfast, said Mokhtar.

Larbi stood up. I'm going to the city, he said.

What for? they said. Don't go.

Good-bye. He went out and walked along the road. At eight o'clock in the evening he got to the town. He walked directly to the house where he had met Khemou, and knocked on the door.

The woman let him in. Khemou was there, and so were two of the other women who had been to the country. Khemou seemed surprised to see him.

Come out for a walk with me, Larbi urged her. We can't talk here.

Wait while I get my djellaba.

A minute later they stepped out together into the alley. They started to walk up towards the market, but they had not gone very far before a man waving a bottle staggered out of an alley and

92

blocked their way. He seized Khemou's arm and cried: Where are you going? As she wrenched herself free, Larbi pushed the man's chest. He swung the bottle at Larbi's head, but Larbi ducked and knocked him down. The man's head hit the pavement in such a way that the blow killed him.

People began to gather. Larbi turned to Khemou: The police will be here now, he said. Go out to Mohammed's farm and tell him what's happened. He handed her some banknotes. Here. You need money. You sleep with men to make money. Take this and don't go with anybody. When my father hears he'll know what to do to get me out of it.

The Spanish police arrived and took Larbi with them to the comisaria. He stayed there two days. Then they put him into Malabata Prison. They did not give him a trial, but they promised him one in a year or two.

Khemou took a taxi straight to Mohammed's farm. She told the story to Larbi's friends, and returned to the city. Then all four of the youths hurried up to the village and gave the news to Larbi's father and mother. In a few minutes the entire tchar knew what had happened.

The following day Larbi's father and a good many neighbors set out on horseback to the city. They went to Malabata Prison and saw Larbi.

What does this mean? demanded his father.

This is what you wanted to happen, Larbi told him.

His father went out and found a lawyer, and paid him half his fee. You'll get the other half when my son is free, he said.

I want to hear the whole story from your son, the lawyer told him.

He went to the police and got the report on Larbi's case. You didn't tell me your son was married, he said.

He's not.

He told them he hit the man to protect his wife. You must go with Khemou and make out marriage papers. Have the notary date the marriage a year ago. It's the only way I can do anything for you.

Larbi's father and the four friends went to the brothel where Khemou worked. They took her with them to the courtyard of the notaries and had the papers made out as the lawyer had instructed.

When the lawyer had studied the false papers, he said: Everything will be all right. I'll do the work. You can go home.

Three months went by. The lawyer was still working on the case. Finally he got it to the court, and Larbi stood before the judge, and so did Khemou.

The lawyer spoke for a while. Soon he said: Larbi, will you tell what happened?

Larbi said he had been walking in the street with his wife when a drunken man had attacked them. He had pushed the man and the man had fallen and hit his head.

When he had finished the story he sat down, and the lawyer went on talking for a long time. At the end, the judge gave Larbi a ten years suspended sentence. You may go home, he said.

Larbi was overjoyed. He ran to kiss his father's hand, and he kissed his mother and shook hands with his friends. And he and Khemou walked out of the court together with his family. They all returned to the tchar.

Larbi's father and mother disliked Khemou and always spoke of her as the dirty woman. Now that she was married she had given up alcohol, but she still liked cigarettes. One day his father came into the house and caught sight of Khemou with a cigarette between her fingers. He walked over to her saying: Allah! Allah! Allah! How shameless!

Is something the matter? said Khemou.

You don't know what's the matter?

No, she said.

You really don't know?

How could I know? What is it? What's the matter?

And even though I'm in front of you, you go right on smoking? Have you no sense of shame at all?

She laughed. But a cigarette's not shameful.

Ah, so it's not?

No. I thank Allah I don't do anything worse than that.

My son is a decent boy, and we are a good family. I won't have him living with a whore who smokes cigarettes.

Khemou looked at him. You know, sidi, you're an old man, and you talk like the people of another century. Your words don't mean anything now. You're old. You should be praying to Allah, because you haven't got much time left. You should be asking pardon for all the things you did years ago. But we're still young. What we do can be forgiven.

No, lalla! he cried. I won't have you smoking in front of me.

You've got to show respect.

You're not a saint or a mosque, you know, she said. You're just a man.

You say that? he cried. You tell me that?

Yes. And something else. I haven't been a whore these seven years for nothing. I knew all about you the first week. And don't try to change me, because it won't work.

The old man ran out shouting for Larbi. Larbi was in the garden. He came running. What's the matter, Baba? he cried.

Your wife is smoking!

Yes? Is that bad? She can smoke or drink for all I care. I love her anyway. You're not married to her, Baba. If anyone's going to stop her, it's going to be me. But I buy the cigarettes for her myself. We smoke together. I want my wife to be free and enjoy herself. I don't want a statue in front of me. This is our time now. Your time came and went long ago.

I see. You can move out of the house, then, said his father.

If you don't want me here, then give me my share of the farm.

You have no share.

I have half, Larbi said.

Nothing. Just take your things and get out.

Larbi got his clothes together and put them onto a horse. Let's go, he told Khemou.

His father came running. Where are you taking that horse? he cried.

I'll bring it back when I'm finished with it. You've got dozens of horses. You won't need this one for a day or so.

He lifted Khemou onto the horse, and he followed behind on foot, and they went without speaking, to Mohammed's farm. He was there alone.

I've fought with my father and I have nowhere to go, Larbi told Mohammed. I'd like to stay here with you.

Of course.

For four months Larbi and Khemou lived at Mohammed's farm, helping him with his work. One day Larbi's brother Abdeltif arrived, saying that their father was very ill and wanted to see him.

Larbi set off up the valley with Abdeltif. When they got to the house they found it full of relatives. Larbi's mother sat with the fqih and the moqqaddem.

Salaam aleikoum. Larbi went to his father and kissed his forehead.

Larbi, son. I'm sorry.

Everything's all right, said Larbi. You called me to give me the share I asked you for?

The fqih and the relatives cried: You see your father dying in front of you, and you can say such a thing?

Larbi paid them no attention. Why did you send Abdeltif for me?

Because I'm very sick, said his father.

Allah will cure you, Larbi told him. Then he turned to the others. If he dies, Allah will see to it that he has a good death.

His father told the fqih: I want to give half to Larbi. The other half will be divided between Abdeltif and my wife.

They began to write this down. But suddenly Larbi interrupted them, crying: Forgive me, Baba! He leaned over his father, and the old man reached up and embraced him with both arms. And he died with his arms around Larbi, hugging him so tight that the relatives had to help release him.

Then the tolba came and began to chant, and they carried Larbi's father to the cemetery.

Larbi took charge of the farm, and for the first time the men who worked there began to receive wages at the end of the month.

Khemou did not mind living in the country. Sometimes Larbi would look at her and think: They say that whores make the best wives, and I believe it.

THE WELL

I was nine years old, and we were living in Emsallah. My father did not like it there, because it was noisy and full of people, and there was no fresh air. And so he found a house in M'stakhoche, with a large orchard full of trees. Orange trees, pear trees, plum trees. And there were three wells. Two small ones and a big one.

One day I went with my mother, out to the big well, to help her draw water. As I was filling my pail a snake stuck its head out of the rocks in the side of the well. Its head came out, and it stayed there, watching us. And it made me happy to think that there was a snake living in the well.

My mother took her pail of water back to the house, but I stayed there. I picked up a few stones and tossed them into the well. The snake went between two rocks, into its hole.

After that I kept going back to the well. I would get up in the morning, have my breakfast, and run out into the orchard to sit by the edge, looking down into the water. I would see my face down there. The water was clear, and I could watch my reflection in it. I would drop pebbles to see my face begin to move back and forth. This was what I loved most of all.

Sometimes I would see the snake. It would come out from between the rocks and stay like that, half outside and half inside its hole. Once in a while it would come all the way out and swim around on top of the water.

One day when I was sitting there, it seemed to me that I heard a voice. It was saying: Look out, boy. Get away from that place.

What did I think? I said to myself: it must be a neighbor. Or it

97

could be somebody else. But there was no one around. I began to play again and forgot about it.

The next morning I played by the well, and again in the afternoon. And then as I was sitting there I suddenly felt a blow in the face, as if someone had struck me. I turned my head around in every direction, and there was no one anywhere.

My head began to hurt, and my body felt heavy and soft, and I was cold. Then I started to sweat. I walked back to the house.

Mohammed! my mother said. What's the matter?

Listen! I was sitting on the edge of the well, and somebody hit me. And nobody was there. I'm sick. I feel cold.

Come, she told me. I'll put you to bed, and you can rest a little.

Yes. I got into bed and lay out flat. Cover me up, I kept saying. Cover me more. And she piled blankets over me.

After a while I began to feel hot, and I was talking to myself, like a man who has gone crazy. I did not know what I was saying, or what I was doing, or what was happening. I could not eat. All I wanted was to drink water, every little while another glass, another glass.

The next morning when I woke up my face was crooked. My mother began to cry and say: My son is going to die. His face has gone to one side. What shall we do?

My father picked me up in his arms and carried me out to the doctor's house. The doctor tested my blood and found that it was healthy. He looked at my body, and it was strong.

The boy has nothing the matter with him, he told my father. I don't understand where this trouble comes from.

He gave my father some pills for me, and then my father carried me back home.

Three or four days later a Djibli woman came to visit my mother. Lalla Khemou, she said. I've heard about a fqih. He lives in the Andjera country and he could cure your boy.

Yes, Lalla, my mother said. Tell me. That would be a great favor you would be doing me.

In the afternoon my father came home. Ya rajel, said my mother. A Djibli woman was here, and she told me about a fqih in the Andjera who can help the boy. What do you think? Can we take him there and put ourselves into Allah's hands?

Yes. We can go, he said.

The next morning we got into a taxi and went, all four of us, the

Djibli woman, my mother, my father and I, to the mountains. I was sitting on my father's lap.

When we found the fqih's house my father knocked on the door. The fqih came to answer. Sidi, said my father, I have a boy who has been struck by a djinn.

Ouakha, sidi, said the fqih. Let us deliver ourselves into the hands of Allah. With his help perhaps he can be cured.

The fqih took me inside, and my parents stayed outside. He led me into a dark room, and put me down so that I was sitting in front of a brazier with a fire burning in it. He had holy books, and the Koran, lying open on the floor. He threw some bakhour on the fire. It was benzoin of two colors—white and black. As it burned it made a sweet smell.

The fqih begins to read. He reads. He reads. He reads.

And I can't understand anything he is saying, and I don't know what he is doing. I am just there, sitting like a stick or a stone. Or like an animal.

When he has finished saying everything, he lifts me and wraps me up in a white cloth, and carries me out of the room. My father takes me in his arms and goes with me to the taxi.

In two or three days I shall come to Tangier, the fqih tells my father, and finish my work on this boy.

Three days later he comes down to Tangier, and he has with him two black cocks. He comes to our house and spends the night, and in the morning, before the sun is up, he and my father take me out. The fqih holds the first cock over the well, cuts its throat, and lets the blood drip into the water. Then my father picks me up and holds me by the feet, head down, over the edge of the well. The fqih cuts the second cock's throat, and all the blood runs into my mouth, and then falls into the well. While my father is holding me there, the fqih begins to read. Then they take me and carry me inside the house. After my father eats breakfast with the fqih, he pays him.

Let us ask Allah to help us cure this boy, says the fqih.

To me he says: Allah y chafih.

If it is Allah's wish, he will be cured, my father says.

You must not be afraid. He will be healthy again. But keep him away from the well.

The fqih goes away. After four days, my face is straight again. My mother and father are happy and the family stops worrying about me.

A month or so later I was playing with some boys who lived in the neighborhood. Suddenly I said: Let's all go and fill up that well with the rocks.

We began to bring rocks from everywhere, and throw them into the well. Day after day, for a long time we worked filling it, until the rocks were in it up to the top.

On the day of the Aid el Kbir everyone was busy getting ready for the feast. My father brought out the sheep that was going to be sacrificed. I stood there watching while it had its throat cut. The sheep began to shake and the blood came out, and I fell over onto the ground.

They picked me up and carried me inside. They dropped bakhour onto the coals of the fire and sprinkled water over my face. And they put a key in my hand. When I woke up I began to tremble.

Tremble. Tremble. Tremble.

For three days I was sick. After that I stopped trembling.

The next year on the Aid el Kbir I did not want to be there when they killed the sheep. I went out, and I stayed out until I knew the sacrifice was finished. Then I went back home.

Five or six years later, when I was much bigger, a neighbor of ours had a son born to him. And he bought a sheep to sacrifice, so he could give his son a name. Every man has to do this, so that at the moment he cuts the sheep's throat he can say: Bismillah Allah aqbar ala Mohammed, or Mustafa, or whatever he names his son. But this poor man had no one to help him do this. And he came to me and he said: Mohammed, the only one I can find today to help me is you.

I said: Ouakha, Si Mokhtar. I'll help you.

The idea that anything could happen did not come into my head. I thought that the trouble I had had when I was young would be gone by now. I went with him and held the sheep by the legs, tight, and with the other hand I took its head. The man picked up the knife, put the point on the sheep's throat, and then he said: Bismillah Allah aqbar ala Mustafa. And he cut the sheep's throat. He pushed the knife in front of him hard, and drew it back once. The blood came out and hit my arm. It felt hot. And it kept coming out, coming out. I felt dizzy, and I had a fog in front of my eyes. I was holding on to the horns, and then my head moved down to one side

100

and I fell on top of the sheep. It was lucky that the man was beside me. He lifted me up quickly and carried me inside his house.

When I sat up I felt ill, but I knew it was just nerves. The neighbor said: Forgive me, Mohammed. I didn't realize that you had trouble with blood. It must be from a djinn. Only djenoun can do that to you.

It's nothing, I said. I'm all right, hamdoul'lah.

Some time went by. One day I was with six men who had decided to buy a sheep together. Each one would pay for a part of it, and it would come out cheaper and better for all of them than buying meat in the market.

They were holding the sheep, ready to kill it, and I was just standing there watching. I did not want to go near. But as soon as they cut its throat, down I fell.

One of the men was older than the others, and he knew what to do. When I fell down, he ran and got a cup. Then he filled it with blood that was coming out of the sheep's neck, and when I woke up he gave it to me to drink. And I drank it, and I felt warm and happy inside, as though nothing had happened. I was not trembling. I stood up, and I was feeling very well. I was not even weak.

Are you all right?

I said: Yes, thanks to Allah.

My son, he said. Something must have happened to you before this.

Yes, sidi, something very bad happened to me once.

I know. From now on, whenever you are going to be in a place where there is blood, all you have to do is drink a little of it, and the djenoun will not be able to take hold of you. Because if you let them do that some day they can kill you. Or they will shrivel one of your arms, or let one side of your face drop, or leave you only one eye to see through, or make you go crazy. But now you know what to do. If it makes you sick to look at blood, the only thing to do is to drink it.

101

THE HUT

In the Beni Ouriaghel country lived a man who owned many cows and a vast tract of pasture land for them to graze on. His son Mohin took charge of the animals for him. The youth went out with the cattle in the morning and stayed with them until sunset. So that the hours he spent alone out on the hillside might pass more swiftly, he smoked kif throughout the day. His father would often say to him: The best thing for you is to go on living here at home. Take care of the cows for me, and I'll give you something now and then.

To Mohin, watching cows was the worst sort of life any young man could have. He and his friends had built a shack outside the village where they all met each afternoon. When the day was finished, Mohin would drive all the cows back to their stalls, and hurry down to the cabin where the others were waiting for him.

The cabin was a place that only the boys knew about. There they could do whatever they pleased. There were mountains of kif lying on the floor, which they used both for smoking and for preparing hashish milk. This had a powerful effect for something so easy to make. They would heat the kif in an oven and then roll it into powder while it was still hot. Then they would mix milk with the powder and drink it. Once they had drunk hashish milk they were certain to laugh and sing for many hours. Here in the shack with his friends Mohin was able to forget that he spent his days sitting with the cows.

However, Mohin's father had noticed the haste with which his son ran off down the hill each evening, and one day he determined to follow him and find out where he went. He kept a good distance behind the boy, and when he saw the cabin he stood still. He could hear the young men shouting and singing. Then he hurried back to the village to tell the other fathers.

You wanted to know where your sons go. I can tell you. They've built a shack down in the valley and they're all there in it now.

Several of the men said they must go there right away. They went and got the moqaddem, and he said he would go with them. It was dark when they set out for the shack. Long before they got there they saw a huge fire burning. As they drew nearer they heard the drums. Then they saw that some of the young men were dancing around the fire. The others sat in a circle playing drums and flutes. There was a sheep roasting on the fire. The men kept walking, until they were very close.

Suddenly the boys became aware of the men standing in the shadows watching them. They stopped, jumped up, and began to whisper to one another. What are we going to do?

The moqaddem walked over to the boys. Go on playing, he told them. Why did you stop? And so they sat down and began to play again, wondering what was going to happen.

They're going to burn down the shack, thought Mohin. I can save it. He seized a bowl and filled it with the hashish milk. He carried it across to the moqaddem, and because he had the best voice of all the young men, he sang as he walked, and the words were: *Who would make a slave of his son?* The moqaddem, thinking that Mohin was offering him milk, drank half of what was in the bowl. Then Mohin refilled it, and went to each of the men with it, and each one followed the moqaddem's example. When he came to his own father and held out the bowl to him, the man was so confused that he drained it without even drawing breath. Then Mohin took the bowl and sang a song which went: *If only I'd known when I was still in my mother that you were the one I was going to call Father! From there I should have sent up a prayer to Allah: Let me die before I see the world!* When he heard these words the man was too shocked to say anything. The youths looked at one another and smiled.

Then Mohin and a few friends went in search of wood, and brought back the trunks of trees and threw them onto the fire. They cut up the sheep, and all the boys began to eat. The hashish milk was starting to have its effect on the men. They merely stood and watched their sons eating by the light of the fire.

After the youths had finished the sheep, they sat back and took up their drums and flutes again. The flames blazed higher. Soon Mohin jumped up and began to dance. When he was ready he stepped into the fire and pulled out a large glowing ember. He rubbed it over his face, ripped off his clothes and seared his body with it, and then he fell to the ground.

By now the men were full of hashish, and they began to walk away from the fire, leaving the boys to play their drums and flutes. They staggered back to the village without speaking. Mohin's father, having drunk the entire bowl of hashish milk, felt extremely hot, and so he left the door of his bedroom open when he went to sleep. Early in the morning his dog awoke, came into the room, put his paws on the mattress, and began to lick the man's face. He pushed the dog away, opened his eyes, and sat up. He stared at the animal, and wiped his lips with the back of his hand. Then before it could escape he seized it by the scruff of its neck and strangled it.

The man washed his hands, face and mouth, and went out into the courtyard. His brain was still boiling with hashish milk, and when he saw the axe that hung on the wall he took it and went outside to look for Mohin. As he ran through the street he met another man with a scythe in his hand. He called out to him, and the man stopped.

They put something in that milk they gave us last night, the man said. When I got home I went crazy and butchered five of my best cows. And now if I find my son Bouchta, I'm going to do the same thing to him.

Good, said Mohin's father. We'll find them and cut them both into pieces.

A boy who stood in a doorway nearby heard what they were saying. He went running to the shack and pounded on the door. Quick! he cried. You fathers are on their way here.

Mohin seized his sebsi and his naboula of kif, and rushed out of the shack. He saw the two men in the distance, coming over the hill, and called to Bouchta. Together they ran to the river, jumped into the water, and swam to the other bank.

Their fathers did not find them in the shack, and so they went back to the village, thinking that Mohin and Bouchta would return later, and that they would deal with them then. However, neither boy was ever seen again by the Beni Ouriaghel.

THE WOMAN FROM NEW YORK

An American woman came from New York to Tangier on a visit. On her arrival, she went to a hotel in the Zoco Chico. After she had stayed there for a month or so, she began to look for a certain Englishman who lived just outside the city. She got his address, took a taxi to his house, and knocked. The Englishman opened the door. She gave him her name and he gave her his.

Come in, he said, and she went in. He had no idea who she might be.

Sit down, please. She sat down.

What can I give you to drink? he asked her.

Cognac, she said.

There's no alcohol in the house, he told her. I can give you tea or Nescafé.

Well. Tea with lemon, she said.

He brought her tea. While she drank it she talked about herself. The time passed, and evening came. Soon a young Riffian who worked in the house arrived to prepare dinner. The Englishman stood up and said to the American woman: This is my friend El Rifi who helps me. They shook hands, but since he said nothing more to her, they did not speak again.

They had dinner and talked until one o'clock in the morning. Then the American woman said she must be going. She wondered how she would get to Tangier at that hour.

I'm sorry. I have no telephone, said the Englishman. So I can't call a taxi for you. I did have a telephone, but it was such a bother I couldn't go on with it, and in the end I ripped it out of the wall.

Really? she said.

El Rifi turned to her: I have a car. I'll take you home. The American woman put on her coat and went with him to the car in the driveway, and he drove her directly into the Zoco Chico. She got out. Good night. See you soon. And she went into her hotel.

When El Rifi got back to the house the Englishman said: Did you take her all the way to the hotel? Where did you let her off?

In the Zoco Chico. After midnight you can drive in from the port. She's in a hotel that's full of Nazarenes, the kind that wear Moroccan clothes and take drogas. Do you know that woman?

It's the first time I ever saw her.

Where's she from?

New York, said the Englishman.

Does everybody in New York dress like a beggar?

The Englishman laughed. No. They like to live that way. Even when they have money, they like their own sort of life better.

You mean they like to live in dirt? I don't understand them. They start out healthy and clean, and they always end up sick and dirty.

El Rifi had a tape-recorder which he carried with him everywhere. He knew several other young men who worked for the English and the Americans, and they all had tape-recorders. The next morning he packed up his machine and took it with him to the beach. He carried some sandwiches along with him, and sat on top of the rocks looking out to sea. Soon he began to talk into the microphone. He wanted to tell everything he knew about the ocean. He was in the habit of smoking a great amount of kif, and the kif made him feel like talking.

That afternoon when he went to work at the Englishman's house, he found the American woman sitting in the salon. He set his tape-recorder down and asked her: Do you want something to drink?

I'll have some tea, please.

El Rifi made tea and served it to them. Then he took out his kif-knife, his board and his sifter, and began to cut several sheaves of kif on the floor in front of them. Presently the Englishman said: I'm going to the city. I've got something to do.

Buy some mutton, and I'll make a tajine tonight, El Rifi told him.

The Englishman went to the post office to get his mail, and the woman was with him. From there he went to the Fez Market. The woman was still with him. He bought the meat and some prunes and salad, and a loaf of whole wheat bread at Pino's Bakery. And later he stopped at the Soussi's and bought a liter bottle of Gris de Boulaouane. Then both he and the woman carried the things back to the house.

The woman went into the salon and sat down, and the Englishman went to the kitchen with the wine and the food. El Rifi took out the meat and washed it thoroughly. Then he cut it in pieces and put it on to stew. He was a good cook because he enjoyed cooking. That night he made a tajine of mutton and prunes with cinnamon, a very light purée of potatoes, and a green salad. And they began to eat. The woman drank the entire bottle of wine. Then she smoked some kif. When they had finished eating, she began to talk about the man who had been her husband, but she had nothing good to say about him. My family never thought he was the right husband for me, she said.

El Rifi looked at her while she talked, and he thought to himself: She probably comes from a very backward family, the kind of people you wouldn't even spit on. He did not want to say anything, so whenever she spoke to him he smiled and said: Yes.

After a while the woman remarked to the Englishman that she had very little money. I hate living in hotels, she said. It's so expensive. I'd like to find something very cheap and rent it, so I could stay in Tangier as long as I liked.

The Englishman said: I have a furnished apartment you might use for a while if you like.

Oh, no. I couldn't do that, she told him.

Then El Rifi said to the woman: If you want to go home now, I'll take you. He said to himself that he was doing this favor not for her, but for the Englishman. He could not let the man's guest go out drunk into the night and meet drunken Moslems in the street on the way to the hotel.

He drove her to the Zoco Chico, and she tried to kiss him on the cheek as she got out. He ducked and gave her his hand. Sleep well, he told her.

Good night. She went into the hotel. When El Rifi got back to the house, he said to the Englishman: You know something?

What's that?

That woman's no good.

Why do you say that?

She's going to make trouble. For you and for me too. I know from the way she talked about her husband, and the things she said about her own mother and father. She'll talk the same way about us with other people.

Oh, I don't think so, said the Englishman.

A month or so passed. The woman went nearly every day to the Englishman's house. She would stay until it was time to eat, and the Englishman would invite her to have dinner with him. Afterward she would sit talking until very late. One evening, however, she left soon after dinner, and El Rifi took her in his car. As they were driving along the road, she turned to him. Why don't you speak to him about his apartment? She said. Do you think he wants me to have it? Do you think I should take it? Ask him about it. We'd be neighbors, and it would be fun.

You'll have to excuse me, he said. It's got nothing to do with me. If you want to live in his apartment you'll have to ask him yourself. Suppose something happened.

What could happen? Nothing's going to happen.

I don't even trust my own shadow, El Rifi told her. You're a Nazarene and he's a Nazarene, and you both speak English. You don't have any trouble talking to each other. I'm a Moroccan. There's a big difference between me and you.

Yes, there certainly is, she said. Then she said: Why don't we go and sit a while at the Café de Paris?

They drove to the café. El Rifi ordered a Coca Cola, and the woman a Fundador. Then she asked for another, and another. At the Englishman's house she had just drunk a whole bottle of wine. She began to talk. First she spoke badly of her family. I hate my mother, she said. After a time she grew sad.

Don't you want me to take you home? he asked her. I've got to go. I have a lot of work to do.

What work do you have to do at this time of night? she asked him.

I make tapes, he said. She began to laugh, and he saw that she did not believe him. He called the waiter and paid the bill, because she had told him when they went into the café that she had no money.

He drove down to the Zoco Chico and parked the car in front of a leather bazaar. Come and see what it's like where I live, she said.

El Rifi walked with her to the entrance of the hotel. Then he said: Sleep well. Good night.

Don't you want to come up and see my room?

But El Rifi said: I'm sorry. We Moroccans have a special custom. A man can't go by himself to a woman's room. Not in a hotel, anyway.

She stared at him. And why not?

It's a custom.

She bent forward to kiss him on his lips, but he turned quickly and said: Good night.

You don't want me to kiss you on the mouth. Is that it?

No. That doesn't matter, he said. But many Moroccans don't go with Nazarene women. They're not interested.

Her face grew red. She went into the hotel. El Rifi got into his car and drove back to the Englishman's house.

What happened? You were gone for two hours and a half.

They were very interesting to me, said El Rifi. I learned something. These American women who come here to Morocco sell themselves very cheap. A woman comes to Tangier and a chauffer drives her to her hotel and she asks him to her room. What does that mean?

You'd have to go up and find out, said the Englishman. You'd have sat down and talked, probably.

El Rifi laughed. He took out his sebsi and smoked. That woman told me to ask you if she can live in your furnished apartment, and I said it was none of my business, that she had to ask you herself and you'd tell her. Myself, I don't like her. And if you like her and want her to live there, it's your mahal, not mine. And excuse me.

A few weeks went by. The Englishman gave the apartment to the woman from New York, and she brought a valise with a few old clothes in it. She spent every afternoon in the Englishman's house, sitting in the salon, and when El Rifi came he could not work there as he always had done. He was angry, but she was a guest of the Englishman.

One day the woman asked the Englishman why he allowed El Rifi to have the keys to his house. I shouldn't think you'd want him coming in here at any hour he pleases, she said.

It's nothing new. He's had the keys for years. I trust him.

I know what I'd do, said the woman. I'd change the lock. Then at least he'd have to ring the bell.

The Englishman did not answer.

He's a hoodlum, she said. I've asked about him. He's well-known all over Tangier.

If he is, I don't know about it, said the Englishman.

Perhaps the woman supposed that the Englishman would say nothing to El Rifi about this, but she was wrong. When he told him, El Rifi said: That's nothing. Any time you want your keys back, here they are. He threw them on the table. And if you don't want me to work here any longer, we can arrange it so I won't come back. I'm not a slave. I'm free to look for another place to work.

No! said the Englishman. I didn't ask for the keys, and I don't want you to leave. What are you so excited about? Finish your work.

The next day as El Rifi and the Englishman were having tea the doorbell rang. El Rifi got up and opened the door. There stood the woman from New York. How are you? he said. She walked into the salon, and he followed her. Which do you want, coffee or tea?

I'll have a cup of coffee this time, she told him. After she had drunk it, he offered her a pipe of kif.

No, no! I can't! she said.

El Rifi turned to the Englishman. Why don't we go out to Achaqar?

Why not? he said. There's a little café there in the sand where we can sit.

At Achaqar they got out of the car and stood looking at the ocean. The qahouaji came and shook hands with them and took them into the café. They sat down beside the window and ordered tea. Several Nazarene men with long hair sat nearby. Some Nazarene girls were squatting on the floor as they cooked something. The woman from New York went and began to talk with them.

El Rifi looked at the Nazarenes. The men had dandruff in their hair, and their skin was grey with dirt. Some of them had lice crawling in their beards. The girls had pimples and smelled stale, and their clothes needed to be washed and mended. A Moroccan had been cutting kif in the café that day, and they were smoking what he had thrown away.

El Rifi went to sit with the qahouaji. Those Nazarenes, I never saw anything like them, said the qahouaji. One day I looked down and saw them all running around on the beach without their bathing-suits.

That's because they eat drogas, said El Rifi.

What do you mean? What's drogas?

It's some kind of majoun they make, stronger than ours, stronger than everything. They eat it and then they go crazy. And after that they take off their clothes and run around. If the government finds them here, they're going to put you in jail.

I know, said the qahouaji. I got a stick and ran down to the beach. I told them: You can't go naked here. Put on your clothes. Or put on your bathing suits on. And they were very quiet and they all went and put on their clothes.

El Rifi looked at them again. They were passing around small boxes with pills in them, and taking them with their tea. Some of them talked with their eyes shut. They sat there in Achaqar by the ocean, but they did not know where they were.

Let's go outside, said the Englishman. The three went out and sat on a bench in the sun. After a few minutes the Englishman got up and said he was going to walk out to the top of the cliff. When he had walked away El Rifi turned to the woman from New York. Are all Americans like the ones inside there?

No, she said. Of course not.

But most of them are. I see hundreds of Americans every day in Tangier, and they look like these. I feel sorry for them. They've all got some disease, like tuberculosis or syphillis. If you live with filth you catch filthy diseases. And you die soon.

Oh, they like their life, said the woman from New York.

Yes, the way you like yours. You have the same ideas they have.

Who? Me?

Look at those old bluejeans you're wearing. You've had them on since the day you came from New York. You don't want to wash them or change them. You're living in a nice apartment and you don't have to pay any rent. You have enough money to keep clean.

She was very angry. And you! she cried. Who are you?

It's got nothing to do with me. I'm a Moslem. The poorest Moslem is cleaner than most Americans. He doesn't have to have hot water. All he needs is clean water. For instance, I think I'm better than you because I wash five times a day.

The woman laughed, and El Rifi jumped up and went down to the beach and changed into his bathing-suit. Then he began to do handsprings and acrobatics on the sand. When he climbed back up to the café, the woman was still outside on the bench. She looked at him and said: Lots of muscles, no?

111

El Rifi was drying himself with a bath towel. If you treat yourself well, you'll be healthy, he said. And if you don't, you'll get sick. And every time you say something against somebody else, you're not treating yourself well.

What are you trying to say?

I'm trying to tell you you should keep your mouth shut, El Rifi told her. Don't talk about me.

And what does that mean? she demanded.

It means I'll knock you down. Here in Morocco we don't pretend to have respect for women the way they do in America. It's not like New York. We keep women in their place.

The Englishman arrived then and went into the café to pay the qahouaji. When he came out he and the woman got into the car. Her face was angry. El Rifi slammed the door and began to drive them up the trail to the highway.

After that the woman would buy food and take it to the Englishman's house. She would get up in the morning, go to the market, and buy a few grams of meat and four potatoes and a small head of lettuce, and put it all into a plastic bag, and leave it on the table in her apartment until the middle of the afternoon. When she arrived she would say: I've bought the food for dinner. I'm going to be the cook tonight. El Rifi was pleased, because he knew the meal was going to be bad. He told the Englishman: Now you'll see what bad food is.

But what can I do?

El Rifi laughed. It's none of my business.

She would cook the food and give it to the Englishman, and he would eat it because he was hungry. Since she had never before tried to cook, she would open a book of rules and put it in front of her, and try to follow it. But she had to keep running to the book.

She bought every sort of herb and seed they sell in the market, and many were of the kind that are not supposed to be used with food. But she would put a little of everything in and stir it. The Englishman did not enjoy eating these meals. Half the time she bought fish, which he did not like. And besides, the fish she bought was always several days old. Before she began to use the kitchen El Rifi, who often went fishing, would bring back fish that he had just caught and cook it. But when he saw that she came every night, he stopped cooking altogether.

Each night after dinner the woman began to complain about her life. She would get drunk and quarrel with El Rifi. One night she accused him of gossiping about her with other Nazarenes.

I'd never do that, he told her. It's shameful. If I have something to say about someone I say it to his face. The day I want to gossip about you I'll come and kill you with my two hands.

She called him a name in English, and jumped up and ran out of the house. A few minutes later El Rifi, who had been growing more nervous each instant, ran out too, and drove down the road looking for her. He pulled up beside her as she was going along under the trees, leapt out and seized her arm. When she tried to jerk away, he felt like hitting her, but he merely held on to her more firmly.

You're a pile of garbage, he said. There's plenty of filth around, so you won't be lonesome. You weren't able to manage on the street in New York any longer, so you came to try it here. But you won't have any more success here than you had there. Maybe you'll find a dog once in a while.

The woman from New York was crying now, and walking faster, trying to get away from him. It's true, said El Rifi. You bring those long-haired Nazarenes into your apartment. Every day different ones. They sit and drink wine and smoke kif and hashish, and the smell that comes out of them can give you a headache for a week.

She tried to run. There was no one in the road. He shook her arm. Listen to me when I talk to you! And the Moroccans you find in the street and take back to your apartment! Why do you always pick the dirtiest ones?

He let go of her and went back to the car. When he got to the house, the Englishman wanted to hear exactly what he had said to her.

The woman from New York continued to go every day to see the Englishman. If El Rifi came in and found her there, he would bring his tape-recorder and microphone and begin immediately to speak into it, sitting on the rug in the middle of the salon. This made her very nervous. How can he go on talking like that, night after night? Doesn't he ever get tired? What does he think of to say?

The Englishman would laugh. He says Allah helps him, he told her.

I'm trying to write a book, she said. And I get ten words written every month.

But Allah's not helping you, said the Englishman.

113

One day she invited an American from Marrakech to the English-man's house for dinner. She had bought a fish that was spoiled. When she put it on to cook a terrible smell filled the house. But she left it in the oven and served it to them. The next day the English-man had cramps in his belly, and went to see a doctor.

You've eaten some food that's poisoned you, the doctor told him.

When El Rifi saw that the Englishman still felt sick after several days, he went into the kitchen and gathered up all the leaves and stalks and seeds that the woman from New York had bought, and put them into the garbage pail.

Don't go into the kitchen any more, he told her when she came to see how the Englishman felt. I'm doing the cooking again now. If I come in and find you cooking, I'm going to put you and the food both into the garbage pail.

The woman from New York stopped trying to cook for the English-man. She meant to come when El Rifi was not there, but since she never knew when he would appear, she often found him sitting there when she arrived. One evening she came looking drunk and he let her in. She walked into the salon and said to the Englishman: How many years do you get for murder in Morocco?

The Englishman did not know. El Rifi came into the room. I can tell you, he said. If a Moroccan kills a foreigner he gets four years. And if a foreigner kills a Moroccan, he gets twenty years. Are you thinking about killing me? If you are, you'd better do it soon, or you'll be dead before you get out of jail.

She paid no attention. Look at this, she said to the Englishman, showing him a piece of paper. The police say I have to leave Morocco in seven days. What right have they got? Who did this to me?

I don't understand, said the Englishman, reading the piece of paper.

El Rifi went out. When she heard his car going up the road, the woman from New York said: He did it, of course.

Oh, I don't think so, said the Englishman.

The woman had to pack her things and leave. The night after she had gone, El Rifi was sitting in the salon with the Englishman.

I wonder who went to the police about her, said the Englishman.

El Rifi laughed. Nobody had to go, he said. They found her by themselves. And she was lucky to get out before something hap-pened.

DOCTOR SAFI

Safi lived by himself. It was a small village, and he lived the same as everyone else, except that he had a special pleasure, which was to take qoqa. He would collect all the red poppies he could find and carry them home. There he would pull off their petals and crush their two green seed pods in a cup with a stick. He would put a little of the qoqa pulp into the teapot, add tea, sugar and boiling water, and set the pot on the fire. When he took it off he would stuff fresh mint into the top of the pot. Finally he would pour himself a glass of the tea and take some snuff. But his snuff too had qoqa in it. He made a powder of the dried pods and sprinkled it in with the tobacco.

One day after he had drunk his tea and taken his snuff he was resting. From where he sat he could see his donkey in the courtyard outside, and as he looked at it he saw that it was not doing what it usually did. It rolled on the ground in a different way, and there was a little foam coming out of its mouth. Safi got up and went out to it. It was an old donkey and he knew its teeth were bad. He looked into its mouth, and then he pulled out four of its teeth.

You have a few good teeth left, he told the donkey. But it's all right. If I have to take them out too, I'll make you a set of false ones. You'll still be able to chew.

Later, at the end of the day, Safi was sitting with his friends in front of the village mosque. A taleb came by, holding his hand over his face. My tooth! he was crying. Safi, being full of qoqa and still remembering the teeth he had just pulled for the donkey, said to the taleb: Come home with me. I can pull your tooth.

He took the taleb with him to his house. There he told him to sit down on the mat, and he gave him a glass of his special tea. Then he had the taleb take a few pinches of his qoqa snuff.

Soon Safi said to the taleb: Open your mouth. Where's the tooth? Here?

He tied a cord to it. Say *Al-lah!* he told the taleb. Then he yanked out the tooth and gave him a glass of hot water with salt in it and told him to wash his mouth.

How much do I owe you? the taleb asked.

Safi was busy thinking. It's free this time, he told him. Because you're my first patient.

The taleb thanked him and went away. As Safi watched him go, he said to himself: And now I'm going to build myself a clinic.

On his extra land Safi began to build a shack. When it was finished he put benches along its walls. He bought three mirrors and a table to hold the pliers and knives. He filled several bottles with salted water. The room had two entrance doors side by side. On one he hung a sign which read: DOCTOR SAFI——PEOPLE, and on the other: DOCTOR SAFI——ANIMALS.

One afternoon not much later, a man came to the clinic with his wife. She wanted two teeth taken out. Safi was very full of qoqa, and he scarcely knew what he was doing. He tied the woman's hands behind her and bound her legs together before looking into her mouth.

Hold her head tight, he told the man. Then he took a pair of pliers in his hand. Open your mouth. Is this the tooth?

Yes! she cried.

Say *Al-lah!* And while she was saying it he pulled out the tooth. The woman began to groan. He gave her a glass of salt water. Then he reached in and pulled out the other tooth. This time she fainted and fell on the floor.

When Safi saw her lying there with blood coming from her mouth he was afraid. But he went to his room and got some soft soap to stuff into the holes he had left in her gums. When she came to she began to talk to her husband, and it was not many minutes before she had masses of foam coming out of her mouth. This frightened her husband, but Safi merely kept working. He brought in a brazier and some benzoin. With the woman sitting beside the pot of coals, he sprinkled the pieces of benzoin over the fire, and she breathed the smoke. Finally he gave her a glass of qoqa tea.

116

Drink it while it's hot, he told her.

Soon the woman was telling her husband that all the pain had gone away. And Safi said to himself: I've found the right medicine for teeth.

How much? said the man. Safi took the two teeth in his hand and looked at them for a while. The big one will be five rials and the small one two.

Another day a man came and knocked on his door. Salaam aleikoum, said the farmer. I have a cow and I think her teeth are bad.

Come in, said Safi. And bring the cow through the other door. The man led his cow into the office. Safi opened her mouth and looked in. He could not tell whether anything was the matter or not. He got a piece of bread and spread it thick with qoqa paste. After she had eaten it, he opened her mouth again and began to tap her teeth one by one with a hammer.

There's nothing wrong with her teeth, he told the farmer. Here's some medicine for her. She'll feel better. He gave the farmer a mass of qoqa paste.

How much do I owe you?

A rial and a half.

The man paid and left. When he got home he gave the cow the qoqa and put her in with the other animals, but the qoqa soon got into her head. She began to kick and bellow, and she attacked the other livestock. When the farmer went out to see what was happening, she came running at him and tossed him into the air. Then she turned and pushed one horn into his thigh and began to tear open the flesh. The neighbors came running and tied the cow up.

We must take him to see Dr. Safi, said the neighbors. They carried the farmer to the clinic and Safi looked at his leg. He got a needle and some heavy thread. Lie still, he told the farmer. I'm going to sew up your leg.

He put the needle into the man's flesh, and the man began to yell. He pulled it out, and went to get him a glass of tea. When he had drunk it, Safi brought him another glass. He tried the needle again, and the man yelled again. I've got to find the right medicine for things like this, Safi said to himself. He brought a handful of powdered qoqa and a third glass of the tea. Put the powder into your mouth and drink this, he told him. He waited for a quarter of an hour, and the farmer fell back asleep. Then Safi sewed up his leg. Now take him home and put him to bed.

The neighbors said: How much do we owe you?

This was a lot of work, Safi told them. I used a lot of expensive thread and broke four needles on him. So I'll have to charge you twenty rials.

Each neighbor gave a little. They paid Safi and carried the farmer home. When they had gone, Safi went and sat on his sheepskin to enjoy himself. He poured himself a glass of tea and ate a spoonful of qoqa paste as he drank it. He was thinking that now that he was a doctor he must go down to the city and buy medicines. I've got to make a list of what I need. He got up and brought a board to write on and a pen made from a piece of cane.

The first medicine I need is red pepper. And then I need cumin and black pepper. And henna. He went on writing out the names of many other things he wanted to buy. Soon he got onto his horse and started out for the city.

He tethered his horse in the fondouk. Then he went to see a man who had a stall inside the gate. Give me two pesetas worth of red pepper and two of black. And the same of cumin and cinnamon and anise. He paid the man and went on to another stall. Give me two pesetas worth of rasoul and a bottle of orange flower water, and two pesetas worth of chibb. He paid and went out into the street, where a woman sat on the curb. She was holding an open umbrella over her head, and she had many kinds of resins and powders spread out in front of her. He bought a rial's worth of benzoin. And he went to a bacal and bought a pound of honey, and string and needles.

Before leaving the city he collected three big wooden crates, because he wanted to build benches for his patients to lie on. He tied everything onto his horse and set out for the village.

When Safi was back home again he got to work. He built fires in both of his braziers and put a pail of water over each fire. From the other room he brought a collection of bottles of all sizes. While the water heated he pulled the three crates to pieces and took out the nails. When it was boiling, he put anise seed in one pail and cumin in the other, and left them both on the fire to boil. After they had boiled for a long time, he began to fill the bottles. Then he corked them and put them on the shelf. The rest of the things he arranged in tins, and piled them on another shelf. Finally he built the benches out of the crates, and covered them with burlap bags so they would be comfortable to lie on.

One evening when he had taken a great deal of qoqa, he heard a knocking on the door and the sound of a voice calling. He opened the door and saw a man. What is it?

My wife's having a baby and the midwife can't manage it.

I'll go and look at her, said Safi. He took a bottle of boiled anise and one of cumin, and followed the man.

They went into the man's house. Give me a glass, said Safi. He mixed the anise and the cumin water and told the man to make his wife drink it.

When she had swallowed the stuff the woman opened her eyes and began to move around in the bed. Safi seized her hips and pushed, and the baby slipped out. The woman took the child in her hands and cut it loose.

Everything will be fine now, said Safi.

How much money is it going to cost?

That's the best medicine I have, Safi told him, and it's made of the most expensive materials. I gave you forty rials' worth of it.

I have a young cow, said the man. I can give her to you if you like.

Fine, said Safi. We'll close the deal tomorrow in front of the cheikh.

The man agreed.

The following morning Safi went out to meet the man with the young cow, and together they went to the cheikh. He took the calf back to his house and tied it up with the other cows, very much pleased because it was worth much more than forty rials.

One day a group of men brought the pacha of a distant city to see Safi. He was a man who was always sick, and wherever he went in his travels he looked for a doctor. When his hosts told him that there was a doctor in the village, straightway he wanted to see him, and they carried him on a litter to the clinic.

The pacha was thinking: Maybe at last this one will give me the right medicine.

When they arrived at the clinic Safi was just finishing another large shack he had been building. *Salaamou aleikoum.*

Aleikoum salaam. This is the Pacha of Bzou who has come to our town.

I'm very sick, the Pacha said.

Take him inside, Safi told them. How many of you are there?

There are six of us.

I'll have this room finished in ten minutes. You'll be needing it to sleep in, because you'll all have to stay here until he's cured.

They agreed. Safi finished hammering, and put some mats on the floor. Then the pacha and his friends went inside. Safi followed them, and knelt down to prepare tea for his visitors, and he put qoqa into the tea as he worked. And he set out a plate of qoqa mixed with honey for them, so they could eat it along with their tea.

Then they sat back to drink, Safi said to the pacha: Where do you feel sick?

I don't know. There's no such disease as what I have.

But try and tell me what it's like, Safi said.

The pacha shut his eyes. When I fall asleep I don't know whether I'm really asleep or not, he said. And when I eat I don't know whether I've eaten or not. And if I go out for a walk I'm not sure whether I'm taking a walk or not. Even if I sit still, I'm not certain whether I'm really sitting there or not. And right now, am I talking? Or do I just think I'm talking?

Safi jumped up. What luck! he cried. I've got exactly the medicine for that. I've seen many cases of the same thing, and I've cured them all.

You have? The pacha was delighted.

This man is not sick, thought Safi. He's just rich. And he's afraid of dying. That's all.

He took a pail of water and put it on the fire. When the water began to boil, he threw in a lot of red peppers. And he let them boil for many hours, as if they had been cow's flesh. When they were ready, he took a fine cloth and placed it over the top of another pail. The liquid went into the pail and the pieces of red pepper stayed in the cloth. He filled a bottle with the water and picked up a piece of rasoul, the clay that women wash their hair with. Then he walked over to the pacha.

Ya, Sidi Bacha, he said. Here's the medicine. It's not medicine. Take it or don't take it. It will either cure you or it won't.

The pacha looked at Safi. And what does all that nonsense mean?

You tell me you sleep and you don't sleep, and you eat and don't eat, and sit and don't sit. I'm giving you the medicine for all those things. Drink half a glass of this the first thing every morning and eat a piece of this rasoul while you drink it. And do the same thing when you go to bed.

Good.

When evening came, the pacha decided he would begin his treatment. First I'll put the solid stuff into my mouth and then I'll wash it down with the liquid, he thought.

So he put the clay into his mouth and drained the glass of pepper water. As it reached his stomach he felt fire inside him, burning his throat and his heart. And although he had not got up from bed by himself in many months, he sprang up now without any help from anyone and began to walk back and forth very quickly. His face turned the color of fire and he breathed with his mouth opened wide. Soon he went outside and looked at the sky, and suddenly it occurred to him that he was cured. He called to his friends: It's a fine night! Come out and smell the air!

They all went out and raised their heads and sniffed, and told him that it was indeed a beautiful night. When they went back inside, the pacha sat in a corner for three hours talking to himself. After that he fell asleep.

In the morning when he awoke, the pacha decided that he felt so well he would not bother taking any more medicine. He went to speak with Safi. I'm cured, hamdoul'lah! My health is perfect. I feel like a man of twenty. How much do I owe you?

Speak with your own image, said Safi. You know what your health is worth to you.

The pacha took out a small pouch full of gold coins and handed it to Safi. And he and his friends went out.

Safi was not satisfied with his clinic, because he still had not discovered a medicine strong enough for serious cases where he had to cut and sew flesh. He worked at this each day, and went on mixing things together and trying them himself afterward. One day he picked some datura leaves and dried them over the fire. Then he made a powder of them, and pounded kif seeds in a mortar. He mixed these two with powdered qoqa. He added argan oil to some of this, and honey to some more. The powder that was left he stored away in a box.

Let's see what this does, he said to himself. He took a spoonful and drank a glass of tea. Then he leaned back and shut his eyes.

Three different people pounded on his door that afternoon, and Safi went on sleeping. Night came, and a man arrived with his son to have Dr. Safi look at the boy's tooth, but still he did not awaken.

In the morning Safi heard the donkeys braying and the cocks crowing, and he got up and opened the door to look out. What's the

121

matter with them all? he thought. As he stood in the doorway some men walked past. And Safi said to them: Good afternoon.

It's early yet, they said. It's still morning.

It's not Monday?

Not any more. That was yesterday, they said.

Safi went inside. Aha! he thought. I've found what I was looking for.

That evening a neighbor woman sent Safi a big pot of spinach and a cauldron of snails cooked with tarragon, because she knew he liked those dishes. He was very much pleased with what she had sent him, and he sat down to eat his dinner in a good state of mind. But he had scarcely taken a few mouthfuls when someone began to hammer on his door with great force.

Wait! he shouted. Don't break it down! And he jumped up and opened the door. There were two men holding up a woman between them. They dragged her into the clinic.

What's the matter with her? said Safi. Put her there on the bench, poor thing.

She's dizzy and she has a fever, they said. And her vomit is bright yellow.

Safi put his hand on her forehead, and saw that the woman was very ill. Her eyes and her face were as yellow as eggyolks. He was afraid, because he did not know what to do for her. But he said: This woman has bousfar. We must get rid of all this yellowness. Has she eaten anything?

Not for the last three days, they said.

Snail broth is what she needs, said Safi. He went across to his rooms and brought the water from the snails he had been eating. When he carried it into the clinic he added four spoonfuls of his new powder, and stirred it into the broth.

The woman drank it all, and then Safi gave her a glass of qoqa tea. Ten minutes afterward she was sitting up talking with her husband, and she seemed very lively.

That's wonderful medicine you've got there, the two men told him. We'd like to buy the whole bowl full, if you'll sell it.

Safi looked at the woman's eyes, and was afraid again. But he agreed to sell the men the bowl of powder for sixty rials. They paid him and led the woman away with them.

After they had gone, Safi sat at his table thinking. He thought of his pouch full of gold coins that the Pacha of Bzou had given him, and of all the rest of the money that he had saved. Suddenly he got up and went out to the house of a neighbor who lived nearby. He sold the man his cows and his donkey, and went back home. There he collected his clothes and medicines, and packed everything onto his horse. He looked up the road and said to himself: This is the right way. Then he got astride his horse and set out along the road, leaving his clinic behind.

About midnight two men came to the door of the clinic and began to pound on it. One carried a club and the other carried an axe, and they were shouting for Doctor Safi. When they broke in the door and searched the place, they did not find him. By then everyone in the village was outside the clinic. The cheikh came running.

The man holding the axe cried: Doctor Safi sold me medicine. When I gave it to my wife she went crazy. Screaming, running, and we couldn't hold her. When she fell down, blood came out of her mouth, and then she was dead. We're looking for him. Where is he?

The cheikh waited a moment before he spoke. Then he said: Your wife is dead. Take her to the cemetery and bury her. Then you can marry a younger one. And here's Doctor Safi's clinic for you to live in. You can have it. The house you're living in now you can sell or rent.

The man looked at the cheikh. Thank you, he said. That's what I'm going to do. You are a very good man.

Everyone went home to bed. Safi was still riding along the road in the dark, happy and with his head full of qoqa.

Also available from
CITY LIGHTS BOOKS

M'HASHISH

by Mohammed Mrabet, translated from the Moghrebi
by Paul Bowles
A City Lights classic: ten unforgettable tales by the
celebrated Moroccan storyteller.
"One of the world's more remarkable literary
collaborations."—*The Village Voice*
ISBN 0-87286-034-5 $3.95

THE LEMON

by Mohammed Mrabet, translated from the Moghrebi
by Paul Bowles
The adventures of Abdeslam, a precocious twelve-year old
Moroccan boy who runs away from his home in the Rif
Mountains in North Africa to Tangier.
"A surprisingly effective book."—*The New Yorker*
"The naturalness of the telling is the sort that artists like
Hemingway have sweated blood
to attain."—*The Oxford Mail*
ISBN 0-87286-181-3 $6.95

LOVE WITH A FEW HAIRS

by Mohammed Mrabet, translated from the Moghrebi
by Paul Bowles
Mohammed Mrabet's formidable first novel about a young
man coming of age in contemporary Morocco—a lively
tale of innocence, experience and obsession.
"The absolute simplicity of the narrative
allies the novel with some of the most sophisticated
new fiction."—*Saturday Review of Literature*
ISBN 0-87286-192-9 $6.95